they
dragged
them
through
the
streets

# they
# dragged
# them
# through
# the
# streets

hilary
plum

**FC2**

TUSCALOOSA

FC2 is an imprint of The University of Alabama Press

Book Design: Illinois State University's English Department's Publications
Unit; Director: Tara Reeser; Assistant Director: Steve Halle; Production
Assistant: Alyssa Bralower
Cover Design: Lou Robinson
Cover Photograph: i/Stock
Typeface: Garamond

⊗

The paper on which this book is printed meets the minimum requirements
of American National Standard for Information Sciences—Permanence
of Paper for Printed Library Materials, ANSI Z39.48–1984

Library of Congress Cataloging-in-Publication Data
Plum, Hilary, 1981-
 They Dragged Them Through the Streets / Hilary Plum.
    pages cm
 ISBN 978-1-57366-172-0 (pbk. : alk. paper) — ISBN 978-1-57366-840-8
(ebook) (print)
 1. Social change—Fiction. 2. Suffering—Fiction. I. Title.
 PS3616.L86T48 2013
 813'.6—dc23

                          2012040001

To my brother

Throwing down the pieces of silver in the temple, he departed; and he went and hanged himself. But the chief priests, taking the pieces of silver, said, "It is not lawful to put them into the treasury, since they are blood money." After conferring together, they used them to buy the potter's field as a place to bury foreigners.

—Matthew 27:5–7

they
dragged
them
through
the
streets

## HOUSE RAZED BY BLAST AND FIRE;
### Man's Body Found

A local man died last night in an explosion in the basement of a house at 11 Linden Street. The blast appears to have been caused by a homemade explosive device, according to officials.

The deceased has been identified as Zechariah Berkman, age 29, the lessee of the property.

After the blast fire spread to the ground floor of the ranch house; several beams, a wall, and much of the roof have collapsed.

The explosion occurred at approximately 5PM and the fire was called in shortly after by three neighbors, who stated that they could see smoke rising from the wooded cul-de-sac and, in one case, had heard a report and the sound of shattering glass. No further information on the device has been released; the police and fire department are conducting a joint investigation.

The deceased was close to the source of the blast and apparently died as a result of the explosion itself and not of smoke inhalation, according to a preliminary statement by the medical examiner. Official cause of death has not yet been determined.

A full report is pending.

# A

A recruiting center? This was the first idea, an obvious choice. It wouldn't be enough, of course we all knew this, it would be only a gesture. But we imagined the smoke and stink, the heat, we pictured keyboards popping apart—it would say something. We told each other.

Those nights in that room, all our words, mingling in the fluorescence where moths swooped and died: I found them, wings shuddering, on the table, on the floor in the morning. I nestled them in the compost to whisper among the onion skins and lettuce hearts. The beginning.

A beginning. A. Yes, it was my house where we gathered, my living room with the road close on one side, on the other the hill descending into brambles, deer paths crisscrossing. I got up, fetched the meal or the weed, finally sat on the stool by the table. Our sense of ourselves as protagonists: Ford stretched out on the couch, announcing his every idea; Vivienne in the chair in the corner, her quick replies; Sara arguing from the floor where she sat like the martyr she insisted on being—no, that was unkind; she stroked the dog's head and he loved her. And Zechariah on the wooden chair pulled close to Vivienne, when he was not on the phone pacing the kitchen, his crisp speech floating out to us.

The bowl making its rounds, what is flame is air is blood. We faced one another.

.

Those nights ended, Ford and I slept in the room with no door, only a curtain, I never felt I was rid of their voices. In the morning I walked the dog down the hill, where the stream bank was mud and protruding roots, a violence of spring melt water. The dog hunted out an abandoned deer carcass, a femur with flesh clinging.

A beginning. Ford would say: A plane taking off, that's how it always begins. Or a ship embarks, a city of soldiers.

Vivienne would summon up an opening line, stand to recite it.

Look, Z would say, and unfold a newspaper.

# V

Someone should tell Z's story; I don't disagree; but I won't; how could I? There was no end, which is needed for stories; and I am no storyteller, I insist on this.

I am a woman of sentences.

Of semicolons.

A woman who stops before going on.

I shouldn't be trusted with anything continuous: I am no salmon leaping up a long river. I am a woman of puddles, of nests. A perfect blue egg or a chaos of tadpoles.

I sat in my corner of A's living room as everyone talked, and I waited for the gaps, the depressions I could flow into, brim over. How loosely their logic was looped together, I thought. I would pull the knots tight at their most absurd. The ideas were enormous but the executions just wet explosions, a thump jarring the stomach, then nothing. This is what I thought then, Z at my side, his laughter whenever I desired it; I was victorious.

Z of course could defeat me, anytime. But he did it quite reasonably, a glance over the breakfast table. And then he died.

Who would have known—isn't it fair to ask?—that this was the direction, how we would conclude? Who would aspire to such divination? This is why I won't tell a story, insist a prophecy play itself out. I will keep to my sentences; within the space of a sentence I can hold back. I can earn what I have always wanted: no more than Z's checkmarks next to the best lines. The lines like small revolutions.

So that even now I await Z's applause, sudden and lovely, birds taking flight off a pond.

In the space of my life I am algae and eutrophication. *Then she was sick*, as they say politely.

In bed insane weeks passed.

I recovered; Z waited for me; we went on. But there have been these pauses.

But—weren't we like anyone, a past no one had the right words for, a future we would not wish to know? We armed ourselves: A with her diligence and nostalgia. Ford—I think he chose to be handsome, swathed himself in good looks as I did in irony, then parried from behind, sharp quick jabs. Sara wanted to be merely useful, and after all she wasn't wrong.

And Z?

Z. The times were violent. It's true. If we tried to see this, which in our best moments we did, the mind opened into chasm, and reason slipped down, and love and hope followed after, though they were the best of ourselves—

But that's no story, end only, no beginning. This is what I mean, what I have been trying to say.

# F

Start with the tree in the backyard. Where the swing was when we were kids in what weren't quite the suburbs. Our yard backed up to a swamp, the kind of land that's preserved because nobody wants it. But we weren't far from town; if Jay went with me I was allowed to walk the fifteen minutes to the convenience store, in the summer went and got slushies. Purple tongue, blue tongue. When we were older Jay would buy beer for me there but first make me sit in the passenger seat and listen to his big-brother lecture. Years later he told us he'd hang himself from the tree, and he did. We were on the phone with the VA, all the clinics, everyone all the time. They said, we won't take him, we can't help him until he stops drinking. He won't stop drinking until someone helps him, my dad said, reasonably. He was the reasonable one, my mom shouted or cried.

Then Jay was dead, ending this chicken-and-egg conversation. I don't know how much he was even drinking by then; I found a half handle of vodka under his bed and a thirty-rack untouched in his closet. I think he'd been drinking just enough to go on, then stopped. That seems reasonable, I told the VA when we went to the appointment they'd made for him, which was two weeks after we found him hanging from the tree where he had said he would go. It was a reasonable reaction, I told them.

When we were little, we twisted the swing around and around so it got higher and higher then Jay would shove it in the other direction and I'd spin like crazy, feet out, screaming. All the neighborhood kids came over for our swing ride. One day a kid threw up and we had to stop giving them. One day the swing broke and the branch was ready for Jay.

You could say this is what radicalized me. Everyone likes verbs like that, *-ize* verbs, which show what regular words can do to people. The brother's suicide. But I don't know what it meant, to see his shadow on the patch of dirt our feet had kicked bare as children. And I was against the war already before he came home. Before he threw up in the car because we went over a pothole, and he said, Over there, the bumps were people. Kids even. He said we couldn't stop for them, we were ordered not to stop, not even for kids, because it might be an ambush, so—front tires, back. He wiped the vomit off his face and apologized.

You can't say what something like that would make anyone do, you can only say afterward—well, this was because of that, because you can't think of another reason, because you can't believe how in one moment everything looks like a cause, in another moment an effect. It's true that it did something, but I don't know what and neither does anyone. When I'm dead they might say something convincing and reasonable and wrong. But I saw his shadow, I saw what his eyes had become.

When I moved into A's house and she helped pack my things, later I found that same plastic bottle half full of vodka under her bed, she'd put it there for me, pushed it to the wall. I don't know what she meant by this.

S

I'm the only one who works at the shelter who doesn't wonder why some of the homeless won't come in, why they prefer the streets—wandering, troops losing strength. Many have in fact fought in wars, and even those who haven't tell the stories. They're such accomplished scavengers they can't help it, I think. They collect stories as they collect everything discarded, cans, clothes, boxes—coins tossed at them out of guilt, not hope. I wonder, though, at the ones who say things I know can't be true, I wonder where these fictions come from. I think they may be telling stories on behalf of the dead, that there are a handful of stories they preserve among them.

Often they die in the streets; we're called, the corpse described.

They tell me about deserts and jungles. You wouldn't believe it, they tell me. One man will say something specific about the shine of this bug's wings or how a plant prickled his ankles, and I'll know this must have been his life.

You're a good person, a few men have said to me.

What do you know? I want to say. I give them their retrovirals, I change the gauze over last week's fight. A good person is someone who helps you, but that's a narrow definition. I have been many things. I don't say to anyone that they're all good. I take temperatures, give out clean needles. I talk to the men about carbohydrates, help them care for the feet's wasted skin. When the virus finally takes one of them I am in the crowd around the bed, keeping the tubes from bag to blood from kinking. I cry, too, quietly, at their deaths; I cry for the body that remains. The tarn of shadow above the collarbone, the long-fingered hands that played cards, grasped my arm. The teeth.

I make them all donate their organs, I make them sign the cards. Don't waste, I say, and I joke, this is your chance at immortality. But many of them still believe in heaven. And most of their organs can't be used.

I live my life forward. I don't regret. I won't haunt the past's landscapes: A's house in the woods, I sat on the floor of the living room though everyone always offered me a chair. I sat and rubbed the dog's head. It is another life.

If I try to look back into that room, I can't see it wholly. This is my place now, here, with these men. Not in that room, the five of us in a home made of smoke and words, the place we returned to even the night Z died. I'm not there anymore.

After all, the blood has its own business. Our vessels never meet. The miles of capillaries, breathing in waste and breathing out what they have gathered: they are only ours. This is the fact of our separation. Even in the moments we are closest to union, what we feel is the skin's friction, the soft nerve-filled walls.

# A

A recruiting center?

The four of them looked at me. It was the obvious suggestion. When I said it I wondered if everyone had just been waiting, not wanting to be the one.

How? Z said.

All right, F said. Ask me next week.

Z was looking at him, eyebrows raised.

It's not that hard, F said.

# F

The night after Z died we sat in A's living room.

I'd done this kind of sitting before and A was looking to me for something. There's no skill to it really, I wanted to say, but by then she was crying again. Straightening the magazines on the table, cleaning pointlessly. Vivienne and Sara should have been there hours before. I rolled a joint and went outside to smoke it. A shook her head at me, she started to fight: if the police come, she meant. I walked out to the yard, to where skunks lingered, raccoons eyeing the compost. She stayed inside, watching for headlights.

For months afterward we thought Vivienne would have one of her breakdowns, but she didn't. I've never understood this. It would be easier, I thought—just disappear into whatever it is, stay in bed, check in to some place, *go*. She didn't.

I thought Vivienne's grief would make her even more of a queen but it didn't. She shrank. At A's house she washed the dishes, and not in the old way, where you'd find one dirty glass head-down among the clean, like a sign.

Without Z, two bottles of wine was just enough. This was a new fact.

I grew tired of watching A watch Vivienne. I got drunker.

Come on a walk, I said to A, putting a beer in my pocket and thinking of that stone by the stream in the dark.

Come to this meeting, she said. She was writing a pamphlet.

Pointless, I said.

I'll see you in an hour, she said, that's how long the walk took if you smoked slowly.

Just for that reason I'd come back another way, starting on what looked like a deer path but wasn't, took its toll in jacket, skin. One long welt across my eyebrow that A laughed at then cleaned. I would have avoided the nettles, I said, but it was dark. And it's not true, I wouldn't have avoided them.

Down along the power lines was the thickest stretch. Back behind the church, the community center. You could find a tent or two here in the summer, a good spot for the homeless. Old fire rings here and there as if the men sat and drank together. Under the hemlocks nearby, the shrubs had been flattened by deer bedding down. As if they too had come for the fire, the company.

I came out by the church, I went home.

A would have finished whatever piece she was writing and left a draft for me on the table. She'd rig the house like this, so that you'd go to pet the dog and start reading again about the latest development, that gold-domed mosque.

No point, I said, when she brought up the meeting again. But as she cleaned the nettle stings I told her about a boy: in the hospital after an explosion he was in the same room as his parents, but they left without claiming him, still showing everyone the pictures, he no longer looked enough like himself.

You could have been a doctor, she said to me, plenty of times.

I could have. But I had my reasons.

•

I had my reasons, I think this now: I go to the lab, I come home. I had my reasons, I want to say to the protesters. Every few months they gather outside the lab again, spend a few days shouting, waving posters of rabbits and monkeys. But every day there's fresh food and water, I want to tell them, the whole place smells like fresh cedar. It's someone's job just to come in and change the bedding cage by cage. The mice caged together—I want to say this to them—never fight, and they sleep piled up warmly, you have to lift them away from the softness of each other. I don't know what they know of the loss of each other.

I don't mind the scratching, their claws in my palm. I think it's something the body knows, that feel of feet and whiskers arriving just before death, I think it could be a comfort.

When I stole from the lab in those days I felt the animals watching me: watching me doctor the supply logs, sidestep the security cameras. This wasn't any kind of belief: they're nocturnal, their eyes were all open in that dark room.

The four of us in a room—just that there had been five.

# A

The first place I chose was the woods where I was young and my brother used to chase after me and my friends, set off small firecrackers he'd gotten somewhere illegally. The ground snapped and dead leaves flew. There was smoke and we screamed. He laughed and laughed. The woods were endless. Toads among the leaves, snakeskins. Deer and trees the bucks rubbed raw in fall. A hawk screaming, five-toed print of a fisher fresh in the mud, I could picture him hooking the fish in that stream, near the rock slide, near the crayfish, my childhood.

Sara thought I was being sentimental, telling these stories. Or worse, that I said all this just to impress F, leaned my head against the wall and talked about the wet rustle of that forest, the moss thick and slippery on the rocks we hopped over, hiding from the hunters and their spoor of Bud Light cans. We left the woods holding armfuls of beer cans to our chests, fresh and still smelling or old and slug-covered. But I spent every afternoon there—if you can't feel something for that, can't be bothered to care for where your life was lived, its freshest hours, what hope is there? I asked Sara this. She had her stern look.

F and I planned everything. I was surprised by his willingness. This is where we'd go, all the neighborhood kids, I said. I thought he'd laugh; it seemed laughable. But on the map the green of the park stretched—only chopped into by the town's thrusting spur—all the way to the mountains. A wildlife corridor, a kingdom. They were draining the swamp outside my old town to build a development. Hacking at my woods and even the woods more distant, which we only ventured into that time that girl was lost and all the kids in town went to look for her, though we could have gotten lost too, we were barely older, and above us a helicopter throbbed, and we were in parts of the woods we'd never seen, and the crickets sang thickly and the bullfrogs and the sounds pressed in on us and the air. We were scared and we sweated. We raced each other back out. They found her after ten hours and she was fine.

So one night we went there, F and I, drove through the old town and into the development. I hadn't been for years and my old neighborhood was more ramshackle than I'd realized. It had looked different against the tangle of trees on the outskirts of town than when the new houses went up, their pools and basketball-court driveways. I couldn't see the rocks and wild grapes of my childhood. We could just smell the grapevines near the field they'd cleared for the development, where dead wood bowed.

Okay, F said. We were wearing all black, and I felt stupid, but we were hard to see in the night, slipping in mud among the backhoes. Among the frames of houses, the concrete basements where an entertainment center might be someday, or an unused tool bench, or stacks of things that in the end no one wanted. We laid out our little bundles, started their timers, and left.

In the morning in the papers the beams were singed and ugly, in places sagging or split, in others fallen completely. The beams would have to be cracked from their joints and replaced, or the whole pulled down, I didn't know how they'd do it. The pictures in the newspaper were hard to make out, newsprint and the black of burned wood. I could smell the wood and hear the snaps and thuds of the fire. In that moment I was happy.

We were gone in the morning and we were scared but no one ever thought of us. No one thought of the kids who had played there years past, who they were now. We didn't do any good: the woods had already been cleared, the land bought up years ago. But something in the dark, in the rush of it. I kept looking down at the mud, at the foundation, trying not to fall. We didn't have flashlights. The backhoes shone, mud on the shovels. I remember the smell of my woods. Sometimes in my dreams I'm somewhere like this, where mice rustle under dead leaves, then there's smoke and we smile.

# F

Someone has to clear the fields, I'd say to A, don't you see? But she said: That's your vision, not mine—and you're no farmer, you know, you're no sower of anything.

She was in one of her moods, crossing everything out, turning her back to me to answer the kettle.

But other people will be, I said. Don't you understand? If we—

Your rhetoric—she slammed the kettle down and heaped sugar—is dangerous. I don't want to be part of it.

I would try to write it myself then, whatever it was. I would call it a manifesto just because A hated that word. But I knew later she would read it over, marking it everywhere, and in the end it would be hers, unmistakably.

What I want to say is—I started telling her but never finished.

But something. The body in which we all live. We all knew the photographs: the man hooded, teetering, wires dangling from his outstretched arms. They weren't going to electrocute him, they said, it was only to scare him. A sizzle on the tongue, nipple, cock. The places we're most ready to receive one another. People always ask how they knew to do this, but who wouldn't? Who doesn't know that where pleasure is felt most is the worst, the best place for pain? If I'd been in that prison—and couldn't I have been, how many recruiters called after Jay went over?—I would have known. I would have watched for hours, the man's arms open and trembling.

What I want to say is—and I tried to explain this to A—we touch the wires together here, in the sites of our connection. To say that we can't deny one another.

A wouldn't write this.

# S

Everyone always thinks that I'm fine, I'll always be fine; people have always thought this of me. But it's just that I know—well, time moves forward, death ends everything. If nothing else nursing school taught me this, every day. Each pathway, the messages traversing each synapse. The organs are softer and smaller than I had imagined. There are so many ways to destroy them.

Our memories are not to be trusted—twisting stories together, lighting them so that we'll watch, distracted, again and again. So that even today as I work in the shelter, as I prick a finger, check the blood sugar, all of them—Viv, Ford, Z, A— rush through me again.

Before the shelter I worked for a while in a mental health institution. I thought after Vivienne that I would be ready for it. I had held her by the wrists, I'd heard the things she said. Z came to see her and she hated him then too, she swore at him and he couldn't bear it. I was patient. I had cool washcloths and when I needed to, I could restrain her. I learned to find her vein with the needle immediately. I could find it even now, I think. If blind I would still know her thin wild arm.

I watched how memory left her. Then the present is terrible. I have seen this come to so many of them, they do the same thing again and again, they try to escape from time. But aren't they free of it, for a moment, when the memory darkens? What Vivienne used to say. She talked for hours. There was no order. In this way for a moment she defied death. She didn't move forward; she didn't look back. The present stretched on and on, her back arching, her mouth howling. I didn't want to sedate her: she was so alive.

I left the institution. I saw her too often in the wide whites of eyes and the grasping hands, straining at the ceiling, the light, at I don't know what, and after the shot the fingers curling inward like drying wings. I saw that they would never be like her, they never resurfaced. They smiled at me one day and the next their faces were slack and unreason had its way with their muscles. I couldn't stand it. Here at the shelter sometimes people get better, and even if not, they know my name, their own. They have histories, even if their histories are lies.

# F

Every day I followed the war. When Jay was over there I followed him, and when he was gone I followed the war. This need is what Z and I understood in each other.

We had to seek the pictures out. The papers didn't print them. Bodies in ice, waiting for burial, parents, children, organs skin had pulled back from. Slivers of glass lodged in the face. Doctors and nurses hung bags of blood and the beds kept filling.

We had to seek all this out. In the papers instead we saw soldiers towering, the sand or city a backdrop.

Once you saw the pictures there was no way not to do something. This is what I've always said. But almost everyone did nothing, it was that easy. So when I said this, people didn't understand. They looked at me and had their opinions. They might claim we had something in common, so that they could say of me: this is right, this is wrong. But I lived somewhere else. I dug my hands into the ice, I heard the planes skimming over. I heard the explosions, and that was enough. There was more than anyone could do. People clipped and bandaged. They filed papers for the dead. This wasn't enough. That's a simple feeling, I think, not hard to understand.

# A

One night, early on, F came up from the basement, eye-brows singed and hands shaking. I wanted to laugh, but swallowed it. He went to the sink and poured a glass of water, which spilled down the front of his shirt as he drank. I laughed. Fire's already out, I said, pointing to his wet shirt, and he turned toward me. He ran his hands over his face. It didn't work, he said, and I nodded. He couldn't quite smile.

You should just pluck out what's left, V said, appraising his eyebrows. You look ridiculous.

I'll shave them for you if you like, she said.

He didn't agree, though the ends of some hairs were black and crackled, dust of them brushed off on the fingers. For weeks when F went to smoke V held the lighter far from him, taunting. It was almost maternal, how she arched her hand between him and the flame, how she pulled the hair back from his forehead to inspect.

The problem's not that you fucked the charge up, she said

to him. The problem's that no one will listen to you until you're good-looking again.

# S

The other day at the shelter we had a young woman, twenty-seven, who'd slit her wrists. She'd done it poorly, across the line where forearm becomes hand. You have to draw the blade up, follow the path of the vein back toward the heart. Instead they found her by the river, one hand tossed toward the water meaning to stop the coagulation, but it hadn't worked, or at least not fast enough, not before the middle-aged woman who spends her afternoons in the shade beneath the bridge had found her.

So young, the other nurses kept saying, but I disagreed.

She would heal. She would have those bandages around her wrist for some time. She commented on this when I first spoke with her—what a cliché, she said, looking down at the bright white, clipped and tucked—and I liked her.

How do you get used to it? Viv asked me once. These are people's greatest tragedies and you have to stick them with needles and ask after their meals and their shit and act as if it were all a matter of course. No delicacy in it, no privacy. They hate you, you know, she added as an afterthought—because it's your job to be there, you didn't choose them but they need you.

I did choose them, I insisted to her. This is what I wanted, to be there with them.

And what is there to be delicate about, or private? The girl's sleeves stiffened brown the next day. The half-toothed woman who had run screaming back up to the sidewalk.

And think of that room, the magazines and newspapers piling up. We read everything, but what did we understand, really? I sat on the floor in the dog hair, I'm comfortable here, I wanted to point out, I don't need anything else. When what we were working toward was no more than: a building blown into glass and metal. More than anything Ford wanted to unfold the paper in the mornings and see this. Z nodded, we all did, but Z's ideas were grander, well crafted, another vocabulary. I didn't agree with Ford, but we were kin in a way, we both wanted to live in our bodies and not in sentences enduring. His words were like him: to the point, bodied. You could feel it in his fingers twisting the wires, his words. He and I were alike, we would suffer for anyone. We were indelicate. We wanted the smell of sex, vomit, shit. Fine, cleaning the dried layers from the wrist's newest creases—this was survival. Fine, asking for what we wanted, refusing what we didn't and like children pushing it away, burning and burying.

# A

At Z's funeral we stood in a row and faced forward. People came to shake our hands as though we were family. We could look at them, not at each other. No one said the word suicide, and there was so much to do that we didn't have to have names for everything. Everything had had to happen so quickly, someone had to know which family members and how best to reach them. Someone, not V, wrote notes for the newspapers and alumni magazines.

V stood there as quietly as anyone. I suppose some people would barely have called it mourning. But did we need this word? We thought we could leave it for those who needed it. We were this well-mannered, finishing everything on our plates. Think of the starving children, our parents had said when we were young—no, not really, but that was something parents said. We didn't need much, no ululation, we knew that what had happened would be allowed to be our tragedy. Together we could say what had happened not what he had done. Closer than a lover is the loss of a lover—something V would say.

At the funeral, I thought: war has efficiencies that would have suited Z better. After an attack write the names of the dead on slips of paper, put the papers in soda bottles, put the bottles headfirst in the ground at the heads of the graves.

A rabbi presided over Z's service, which surprised us. Z's parents hadn't gone to temple in years, it must have taken an effort to find someone. We listened to him without listening to the words. We were in the basement of a synagogue, or the building adjoined to the synagogue, a community space, I wasn't sure. V and I had had trouble finding the building, counting and recounting the numbers on the street as we passed; how is it we were going somewhere we had never been?

Driving to pick V up for the funeral I thought things like: over there it's goats by the roadside, plastic bags of sewage, carpets laid out in the marketplace to sell dates from. Here, morning glory twisting up a telephone pole, empty fried chicken boxes, a man shaking his hair out of the window in the morning to dry.

On the news that day they said there had been a car accident in Baghdad. People had run toward it to help, but one of the cars was a car bomb and detonated.

After the service V and I filed out of our row and waited outside for Z's parents. We wanted to duck out of the reception to come, we felt surprisingly like ourselves, our usual aimlessness: the long walks in the woods that veered off in some direction, into thorns that scraped our forearms and ticks I'd have to slide a thumbnail under and pull from V's skin. I may have touched V, then, where Z never did: that slim chasm in the upper neck, the curve into skull and hair, I found a tick there once, its hard small back and the thought of the mouth spitting who knew what back into her blood. I pulled it free, trying to get the head out. I'm not your dog, V said, wincing.

Z: the one to do even things like this correctly. I eulogized. Z, the child who didn't play graveyard tag but made rubbings. The one who always learned, the face you would want to have to the world, words chipped and polished. Not a bottle planted in dirt, not a description to know him by like: his eyelashes brushed the inside of his glasses. In the photo we were shown of the scene, of his body—his hand outstretched, his face turned toward the wall. Z, who died without saying where he would like to be buried, so we should have hidden his bones and challenged each other to find them, looked for them with children and dogs we found in the streets. Because his death was ours, no longer his. We had the last word—sentenced to death? But he can't hear me, so it's no joke.

·

I begin the story again, V beside me, looking down at a toe she drags back and forth in the grass. We wait for Z's parents and think they must be noting which relatives didn't come. Too little warning, I think, and this phrase seems almost funny enough to say aloud, but V's looking down—her jaw muscles shift, but she doesn't speak.

Walking down toward the stream by my house once or twice F and I found a deer skull on the path, lifted it aside before the dog could start in on it. Coyotes split off the jawbones, leave the faces agape.

F had said of Z's parents: they'll want to know everything, and then they'll never want to talk to us again.

You don't even know them, V said.

That spring in Baghdad parents had taken their children to the animal market for the first time in years. The bomb had been placed in a box like an animal, holes poked in the sides. Thirteen people were dead, we saw the photographs, feathers, splinters of cage, fish, and glass on the street stones in blood. One man told a story afterward: walking toward the market he had seen a tangle of guts on the street, picked them up and put them in a plastic bag.

Before the bomb: a boy's face pressed to the glass of a terrarium.

# V

I wish now that Z and I had written to each other, but he was always there; I never had to write. The only letters left are mine, from just after I'd been sick, little notes claiming recovery; they wouldn't let me write too much, do anything with enthusiasm, intensity—too dangerous.

Dangerous how Z lived, then, for he never slowed. Typing furiously, reading everything, his voice rising as he spoke on the phone. The war the war the war. He commissioned pieces for his magazine and was never satisfied with them. Just chatter, he'd say, waving a hand at the screen, slamming books closed. Waste of time.

Now I have become a book myself, by which I mean, something whose choices have already been made. What I mean is—the past is lost to us. Its dreamed-up cities, its false trees of words. There's no way to live among them; touch them and they crumple, or the hand just goes through. The sentences a web stretched over the paths where I walked with A, the dew on its strands destroyed by our passing. I am not even that, not even a twist of silk stretching from twig to tree bark. I am a relic, the simple fact of the past. I am a warning: you will come to mean loss, what time has discarded. Full stop.

I tried to explain this to A: I can't say what the past was, only that it's gone. I can never say something is this or is that, only what it may no longer be. This is why my novels are not novels of history: they loop and loop. In the end either the feet dangle or the whole slips away, free.

Z allowed what I have had of vision: a bud becoming flower becoming petals pressed within a book.

He was always there, steadying, directing nurses, making phone calls, small notes I've never seen. I don't know how he has hidden things from me; I thought that in death we must finally be known by what words we've left. But he evaded this.

I got better. We had our mornings; he typed and I scratched onto paper, old-fashioned, halting. He researched, went to meetings, slaved over his magazine. I would have clapped till the flesh of my palms numbed.

But we didn't recover. The war didn't end. People read, then clicked the window away, tossed out the papers. I saw Z's face as he read the news. I knew then that our peace wouldn't last, for I too was the world, its failures.

He started spending more time with Ford, called me from their house to say good night.

•

The phone rings now, but it's only old friends. The mail arrives. The magazines are filled with chatter, the war the war, they lament. I finish something—but then? I cannot have anything, not his notes in the margins, what he loved, what he crossed out lightly.

I can still see his thin face before me, his mind expanding, and I am dark and provincial; I wanted a flame to burn me out, and he wished to illuminate.

# A

A post office, I said to F.

He was doing dishes and turned, shaking soapsuds from between his fingers. He looked at me, disgusted.

I said: You said, where we connect—and think of the historic importance, the site of the rebellion, the famous poem.

I wanted: one day in one town people opening their mailboxes to nothing, hands reaching to find nothing. I wanted to combat even a sales flyer, a heating bill, an invitation, gold-leafed.

Back then there were reasons to choose the post office, F said. It meant something then.

But I meant something. I wrote. I tried to write. *The illegality of the war demands a*—or *We will no longer stand for*—then crossed it all out.

*The international community has*—
*For the law to have any meaning*—
*What we*—

I'll write a poem, I said to him later, not meaning it. Or a manifesto.

Good, he said. Or he said nothing.

I could have written: That day seventy-four people died on a pilgrimage from one city I don't know to another.

Why don't you talk to Z about it? F said.

Write whatever you want, F said.

I wrote nothing.

S

The new patient wanted to talk, I could tell, but I avoided him. I came up with something each time he began to say, When I was over there... I'd wait for him to pause and take a breath, which he had to often, pained, and then I'd say, Oh, and your commode—anything to shut him up. He would stare at the ceiling tiles, I wondered that there was no trace there of the path his eyes took again and again. He had been in a fight, brought into the hospital from the street, then to us.

I'm no priest, I want to tell them all. I'm no place to put your confessions.

These perverse urges. The only one I had wanted to talk to me was the attempted suicide, who left months ago. But she of all people said the least. Leave us a way to check with you, I urged her, maybe sounding too anxious. After all, I was no one she'd chosen. She smiled. Put a message in a bottle for me, she said, and float it down the river. Use one from those juices you're always drinking, and I'll know it's from you.

A phone number? I asked, a family? But she offered nothing.

I didn't want her story. Not something that would end with: and then the razor, out in the open because that was my only place. Though maybe that's better, I thought—maybe if we die communally we break down faster, back into the stuff that makes us all up. No, I wanted something of her, not her story. Friendship, you could call it. I refuse to be a nurse about everything. Just something of her dry wit, so much like V's, and her hunched stance over the checkerboard, where she played anyone in the shelter who asked, even the lewdest mumbling drunks, who would come forth from their corners and daytime soaps to take her on. She watched the board as though it were the only thing in the world worth her attention.

But she was gone, the new patient was in her room. It's not our fault, I wanted to say when he kicked in his sleep, jerking so he'd hit his monitor, set off his alarm—these things you've seen, it's not our fault.

You have nightmares—one of the older nurses said to him, fixing his pillow. We increased the dose of his nightly sedative.

His mouth twisted. It would have been a smile, sardonic and masculine, if it weren't for the state of his face.

You wouldn't believe the things I've seen, he said.

I wanted to say, You don't know what I believe.

•

Can I get some more water, miss? he asked me, the next time I checked on him.

Sure, I said. We also have juice.

That'd be great. He looked back up at the ceiling.

There's nothing there, I should have told him. You'll always have the nightmares, they all do. I've seen that same look grow old. Men come in after fights like yours, limbs bruised, slit open, thinner than you'd ever think beneath all their layers. There's nothing there.

He told his stories to anyone who'd listen. The old man who drew closest claimed to have Gulf War Syndrome, but I'd heard that man claim just about everything. The new patient shook his hand and I said nothing.

I talked to the VA for him. Purple Heart, they told me, which he'd said too.

How bad's it looking for my face? he asked me.

There will be scarring, I said, the doctors have done everything and now we just wait and see.

What about my vision? Will that come back? His left eye had lost close to half.

No. But you won't lose any more.

You don't soften things, do you?

I like to think I don't give false hope.

I slipped a thermometer under his tongue. When I pulled it out he said, You look like a tough one. You've seen worse than this.

I nodded, adjusted his pillows, his sheets.

It's too late, I wanted to say, but just marked his chart. Whatever anyone could have done, it's nothing.

# A

The women's bathroom, we decided. It was right above important offices: sink water and toilet water would flood them, computers hiss their death throes, water pooling in the keyboards.

Why the *women's*? V had asked, raising her glass for emphasis, wine licked up almost over the rim and everyone watched it, Z reaching toward her wrist. There's so few women in the military, do we have to punish them more? They'll have to walk up three flights of stairs just to pee.

She wasn't more helpful than this.

But Sara helped, and this was surprising, the next day she came over wanting to know more. F laid out what he had on the kitchen table and she asked question after question.

# V

*The war*, we all used to say—as though there were only one, and it was ours. Each generation must say this—but no; most would be lucky to have only one.

This is not the first war we've known, I wanted to remind them, F especially. Z didn't need to be reminded; he knew his history. But I don't even mean history, I mean ourselves, what has belonged to us.

I was a child during that war, thirteen and hideous. I spent hours examining the terrain of my skin, or went days avoiding my reflection, head down as I washed my hands. In the dark I played my fingers over my nose, my chin.

I liked to buy white bread, two loaves at a time, to tear up and toss to the ducks and geese at the pond in the park. I walked along the bank in goose shit, geese crowded me, honking, the bag emptied and it was frightening, their beaks closer and closer.

I bought the bread always at the same corner store; I liked to sit there and read the newspaper slowly, following the instructions, A1 to A7, B3 and so on. The couple who owned the store talked about the war, they came from that country, or somewhere near it, they knew things; I sat close to listen. I knew nothing; I knew the photographs, on the news I saw sand rising in a firm puff toward the sky, black smoke and sand. I remember the pictures of oil wells burning, filling the sky so thickly that I looked at the horizon, nervous, though here it was late fall, gray and nothing but cars heading downtown.

The corner-store owners must have known I listened; perhaps sometimes they spoke just for me. They discussed news they'd heard from family over there; I sat with my chair pulled close. I bought a box of animal crackers and ate them slowly, tiger head and tiger tail, bear, bear, camel.

The war ended quickly, but I didn't forget it. I had known it, I thought; and it seemed this distinguished me from almost everyone, children in school, teachers, people I watched buying milk and a paper. I had known it: at night I stood before the mirror and drew a kitchen knife along my skin, skimming, just enough to break through. I drew my thumb over the red, I drew it over the forearm, the pale soft place, I wet it. Down the side of the thigh, in the hollows. For years this was just another hesitant pleasure.

I pictured words scrolled across me, arabesques, though I wasn't fool enough to create them.

I never told Z anything of this, though maybe this is what one is supposed to tell lovers, these old secrets, everything one has been alone in. But I didn't, and what would he have said?

Z's skinniness always surprised me, so sinewy—he looked almost starved, I told him, which he didn't like. But he went days barely eating, typing away.

I can still see the pictures of that war. I read about sanctions, damaged children. I thought of this as I looked for the kitchen knife, but didn't picture anything as I played it mutely over my wrist, in the winter the taut skin over the shinbone. And I don't think of Z now, my fingers in the dark moving over me. My mind is a sky, I try to think, and want something to push up into it.

S

The heat was dangerous. I must have said this too many times because Ford gave me a look. We'd heard there were a quarter of a million people coming. This is what Viv had said when we left her in a square near the business district, a paved park with a statue of a minister, his stone paunch lichening. From there we walked four blocks east to get to the march. Viv wouldn't come, she was still recovering.

I had said to her that morning: The heat will be dangerous. And who knows what the crowd will be like.

You know I'm already not coming, she'd said.

The four of us said goodbye to Viv and headed across the park. Around us a street theater troupe was gathering, in red, white, and blue spandex and sequins. A man fanned himself with a sequined cardboard top hat. They began a skit, shouting the names of defense contractors, lists of statistics I couldn't make sense of. It was so hot it was hard to hear.

I wish we were one of those groups that rolled signs from

the tops of buildings, I said, looking up at the cool dark windows.

Hot air rises, Ford said.

As we turned the corner I looked back to see Viv talking to one of the theater troupe, a teenager in a red cape on rollerblades. He looked shy before her, who wouldn't be?

The sidewalks then the street thickened with people. Police stood in rows next to the parking meters, sweating.

Fake coffins wrapped in flags were bobbing down the street. There'll be a thousand of them, the guy on the end of one said when Ford asked him. There were eight or ten visible on this street, wobbling a little, the butt of one almost hitting a cop car. We're meeting a few blocks down, the guy said, From above, it'll be unbelievable. He pointed up as though to show us. There were no news helicopters yet.

A was looking up at the sun flashing off the high windows.

The guy shrugged the coffin back up his shoulders and the flag slipped; Ford grabbed a fistful as it slid and pinned it back into the cheap plywood.

You don't let that touch the ground, Ford said. The guy nodded.

We walked toward the march. It was hard even to get in, people were already pushed to the barrier, too close to each other.

Excuse us, sorry, A said, angling through the crowd. She liked to be in the thick of it.

Z's hand was on the inside of my elbow, surprising me.

Nice little show of nationalism back there, Z said to Ford.

Ford turned to reply but the people next to us started singing. Old protest songs—two generations' wars come together, I thought, feeling the sweat of a man's arm, middle-aged and furry, against mine. *I'm gonna lay down my sword and shield*, he sang.

He had a good voice, a church baritone. The front of his T-shirt was already damp.

A group of kids dressed all in black pressed by us, holding up signs, *No meat No murder No war No abortion!* Z smiled. One kid paused so close I could have slid a pinky through the plug in his ear. Lifted and shook him.

The march didn't move forward. We were a mile from the destination, but we weren't going anywhere. Viv had said: The permit was only for ten thousand, but they say it's a quarter of a million already.

Good, A said.

It's going to be fucking uncomfortable, Viv had said, looking at us doubtfully.

The heat is dangerous, I said again.

And it was. Around us people jostled each other to take out their water bottles.

A woman pushed past us, leading a child by the hand, so small she could have been lost among hips, calves, feet. Is there a bathroom, do you know? she asked A, who said something and pointed.

There were no bathrooms, though, no water.

A coffin pushed through, sharp-cornered.

Ahead of us there was a float, blood-colored, and people were singing.

We stopped, we took small steps forward, stopped again. Someone hit Z in the face with a sign; a thin paper cut opened along his cheek.

You're lucky that missed your eye, I said, and took tissues and hand sanitizer out of my bag.

He flinched as I cleaned it. Thank you, he said. His cheeks were so smooth.

When we looked around again, we had lost Ford and A. It was that group of punk kids, I thought; their stupid black in the heat, their dangerous chains. I raised a hand to cover my eyes, tried to spot Ford and A in the crowd.

Are you all right? Z asked me.

Dizzy, I said.

His hand was on the small of my back. Let's get you some air, he said.

We made our way to the barriers, though it wasn't easy. The cop shook his head at Z.

Not well, Z said, and something I couldn't hear.

You can't go back in, the cop said.

Z nodded, guided me around the barrier. We'll get back in a few blocks up, Z said. His hair was sticking to his neck, his cheeks.

I think I only made it an hour, I said, shaking my head, looking at the crowd, which didn't advance, just pressed closer and closer together. We were standing in the shade of a sketchy electronics store.

It's all right, he said. He had taken off his shirt, wet it, and pressed it to the back of my neck. So kind, I thought, and closed my eyes to listen to the people swarming and shouting, the heat hissing, flashing.

# F

I didn't see much of Jay the summer before he left. I wasn't avoiding him, I was just never home. I worked most nights at the liquor store. He worked days, his old job tossing boxes for UPS. We just missed each other.

One night I came home late, maybe three, and he was still up. I walked up to the door in the dark and it scared the shit out of me when I felt for the knob and there was just air. Jay was sitting on the couch, which he'd shoved round to face the open door. That summer for weeks the humidity didn't lift. For weeks you couldn't sleep. If it wasn't the heat it was the crickets. I'd been listening to the crickets as I walked home from the convenience store. I got dropped off there so no one could hear the car on our road, check the time.

Hey, Jay said as I walked in.

Shit, I said, and tripped on the bottom stair. I looked at him but it was dark and the room tilted in time with the crickets. What are you doing, I said, you all right?

Better than you, he said.

It's just been a night, I said. I had one hand steady on the banister. Don't say too much, that was my rule, don't give yourself away. But I was about to say something about the dippers, little and big, how I'd followed the big one home from the corner like people had—when? I don't know. Something about the points of light as though poked through the darkness, the only thing keeping the summer from suffocating us all—but I was slow and he said:

Haven't seen much of you.

You should come out sometime, I said, but I said it too fast and it wasn't believable.

Yeah?—maybe he was smiling, it was too dark to see. You don't want your big brother tagging along.

Sure. Or we'll go out just the two of us—

Yeah, we'll do that. You know I don't like the rest of that stuff.

The rest of what stuff?

Whatever you're on right now.

Whatever, I said, we'll go for a beer, maybe this weekend. Before you ship out. Better get it all in, that'll be a long dry spell.

It will.

I ran my hand along the top of the post at the foot of the stairs, worn wood we'd grabbed and swung around our whole lives. You don't really care about that, I said.

About what?

Not drinking, all the rules, you don't give a shit, really.

No, I guess I don't.

That's what I thought, I said. Well, better you than me, I guess.

Good night, I said when he didn't reply.

I slid my palm along the smooth skin of the banister, I can't remember if he followed me up.

# V

*If you know that here is a hand.* Last week I was reading a book scarred with Z's notes; it had been my book first, but what I left stacked by the bed for months, he read, finished, moved on. *Here is a hand.* This line irritates me, my hands aging too soon, arthritic: the flesh sinking from the bones and I think of the stream at the foot of A's hill, banks eroded, how roots must grasp to last through spring, though it's supposed to be a season of beginnings. My knuckles swell like galls and I want to puncture them, hope words will buzz free.

Last week I thought I was getting sick again, but now I think it was only memory. There is one year's illness I hate to think of, the one I will always wish undone. Z and I had just met Sara, Ford, and A, right before my first book came out. I realized I envied them, though they seemed so young, though my novel was about to come out and why should I have envied anyone?

After the book came out I was sick for months, a whole

winter. In the spring I recovered—Z broke into jokes, I remember, surprising everyone.

I was feeling better.

Even the news seemed perfectly alive: A car bomb, a new militia, a name that kept slipping from me, I couldn't hold onto it, like a tune one always sings poorly and no more important. A car bomb, a mosque—

I can see my fingers skimming the newspaper, my lovely fingers, newsprint on the fingertips, the nail gliding under a headline.

I was better, I thought.

I took it slowly; I was wise; I spent some hours every day with a mug in hand just looking through the window, in the early spring looking at what green, what world I could see between the slats of the blinds.

Do you want me to raise them? Sara would ask. Sara came almost every day to check on me, though back then I felt that I barely knew her.

No, I shook my head. I was watching the wind.

I will be wise, I thought.

Z's magazine was just getting started and he read me pieces he wanted to publish; I jumped in, I corrected a loose word, a rattling phrase. I was useful.

The trees outside were still bare and the wind pushed their shadows about on my bed. It wasn't warm but I kept a fan trained on me always. Beneath all conversations, the sound of the fan, the wind. When people came to visit I watched their clothes move just toward me.

Do you want me to turn the fan away from you? Sara asked, but I refused. Its current was in my eyelashes, in the nightgown shifting over my breasts, where Z did not touch.

Z held my hand in his. Or he sat beside me on the bed, legs outstretched, reading.

You look better, A said to me.

.

It was A who told me about Ford's brother, told me so slowly, as though the news would diminish if dispersed over more sentences.

Did you know him? I asked her.

Not really, she said, I met him, once he got stuck at a bar and one of F's friends called, said to come pick Jay up, and we went. He could barely talk but he wouldn't come. F and his friend shoved him hard into the back of my car, and he hit his cheek on the way in and bled a little. The spot's still there, on the backseat, rusty-looking. He was saying something in Arabic, that's all he would say.

What was he saying?

I don't know, she said, I think it was *put your weapons down*, actually. Maybe *or I'll shoot*.

Do people really say that?

I don't know, A said.

He hanged himself?

Yes.

With what?

She looked at me: A belt.

That might not have worked, I said.

They think it took a while.

When she left I realized I hadn't asked after Ford. I was this selfish.

But I had been thinking of the body, of what he had found.

There were so few leaves in that season, there would have been nothing to soften the sight of it, a boy's body. And then the wind. I dreamed of this motion; the feet; hands on the branches; children climbing.

I had been feeling better, but one morning the edges quivered and the light was too harsh; I picked up a newspaper and the words slid away from me, tangled, then were still. Sara came and I saw her fear. I was sick again. I lay down, again. It lasted months and was worse than before. I didn't recover until midsummer. Jay had been buried. Ford was moving into A's house, and by then something new had begun.

I'm sorry, I said to A and to Ford, I'm sorry. Dutifully they visited me.

Sara had taken care of me, I remember the smell of her beside me. I reached toward her and she folded my fingers back into my palm, pressed the hand to my chest. I remember a chatter no one else comprehended, my own.

Sometimes, afterward, people say to me that this could be a sort of price: for art, gibberish. But I know better: both are always there; a mind only grasps one at a time.

This is why I have tried to look closer. So close horizons disappear and I can see only veins branching out to nourish, or a branch that broke in a March storm, tipping newborn birds onto the pavement, necks snapped.

That summer I stayed on the couch for weeks, my hands translucent, useless.

There were all these messages about the new book, there had been interview requests—but it was too late.

·

Jay, Jay, Jay, I'd been saying, they told me. I caught myself still singing this.

Who is he? a nurse asked.

I don't know, I said; really I didn't.

·

Today I walked around the garden over the frost-tipped grass. The trees were trapped in frost, light shone in the frost. I had thought I was going again, I was slipping—

But I was only thinking of how people must hate me, I who took their weeks and months and wasted them as my own. Z never admitted this, never seemed to resent.

Sara's eyes were patient and patronizing. I reached and she thought I was clutching, but I was trying to give back what I had taken.

I was trying to atone, I said aloud in the garden.

Still blood and light sustain me; in me, larvae swell and change.

# F

I had chosen the house where Z died. Z and I needed somewhere to work, A didn't like having everything in her basement. She'd started getting paranoid: pulling at curtains that were already drawn, wondering out loud too often about the neighbors—should she plant more trees along the property line, did her mother still have a spare key?

A had gone back to school by then, determined, this journalism program I didn't see the point of, but she was going to every class. She slipped out in the morning without talking to me. Class was really good today, she'd say later. She would take out a book but then I'd find her lying on the floor next to the dog, making cat's cradles with the yarn I used for my maps. I'm using that, I'd say, and we'd fight like children. She went to bed early, library books tossed on the floor next to the bed where they'd be most in the way. This is the right thing for me, can't you understand that, she'd say if I laughed at her as in the morning she was late to class, looking for her notebooks and pen.

The right thing—this was always what she said.

So Z and I looked for a place, somewhere cheap, few neighbors. He insisted it be in his name.

.

They questioned me while I watched them pull him from the house, or the shape of him, covered. I almost just explained everything, everything I could have explained. What did you tell them? A asked me afterward, over and over. Nothing, I said, which wasn't enough for her.

I don't know what to say, I had said to them, a few times.

Had you seen any of this material in the house? they asked.

No, I said—then thought to add: But I don't know if he ever let anyone in the basement.

Were you familiar with his online magazine? Pretty radical stuff.

Not really, I said. I mean, I looked at it, sure.

Maybe I even shrugged.

There was a computer in there, I said, watching the smoke behind them.

But can they retrieve anything—? A asked after. No, I said. I was careful. And later they showed me the laptop, a grotesquely dimpled shell.

You can go home, they said, we can talk to you later, go on home.

I went to A's.

I cleaned everything that was left out of A's basement, dragged it down to the stream to burn or bury it.

By the morning Vivienne was sitting as usual in her chair in the corner, Sara on the floor, holding her hand.

Seems like there isn't really a way to prove anything, Sara said.

The way he did it, Vivienne said, he meant to take all the credit—

Credit? A said. Credit?

I meant blame, Vivienne said. I meant—you know what I meant. That we'd be free of it. It's true, you can't say it's not.

Vivienne leaned toward me, but didn't touch me.

# A

A gas station, Z said.

You could see it for miles, V said.

That's someone's livelihood, F said. No.

There's insurance, I offered.

Not enough, F said.

But think of the horizon, smudged black as if a thumb has drawn a line in charcoal, like a child's drawing—this was V, of course.

We're not children, Z said. A gas station is the most logical target—he looked at F. You just don't think you could actually do it right, control the fire.

If we're not children, F said, then don't bait me.

Could the gas leak into the water supply? Sara asked.

Probably, V said, All those, what are they, benzene rings floating along.

We could do it, F said to Z. It's not impossible.

Did anyone think it was? V said. It happens every day, don't you read the news, of course it's fucking possible.

# F

I check Z's magazine sometimes, but it's done now too. Whoever had kept it up for a while must have moved on. Tired of deleting fucked-up epitaphs from the comments. So he's gone from there too, nothing even sounds like him.

Gone: not pacing in A's kitchen, gesturing insistently, talking you through the whole history of a thing as if you didn't know it just as well. He could only start at the beginning.

Each sentence a step forward. Write, distribute, organize. Z believed in stages of history he could tick off. One step after another in the kitchen, pivot, turn.

When he was hungry he'd make popcorn on the stove, shaking the pan, the popping arrhythmic. His phone would ring and he'd excuse himself. His phone would buzz on the table, edging close to a beer bottle, and Sara would hand it to him, not looking at the number. Excuse me, he'd say. He was so important—this was how we made fun of him, but it was true, you could see it: in his wrist when he held the phone to his ear, the

blue shine of vein and the crinkling where palm became forearm, like the trace of a stream that had once crossed the skin.
He was never still. Pacing, holding his phone, drumming his
fingers, which sometimes Vivienne had to hold to quiet.

What do I miss?

Our conversations? The war? Every day it changed, every
day there was something to read and fail to understand. Jay
wrote, Jay called, we would map where he'd been, and when
he was dead we were left with newspapers. Today a photog-
rapher raising his camera was shot through the forehead. Yesterday a car was stopped by gunfire then searched, rubber and
flesh stench, a family. Children in the backseat, heads hanging
forward. Every day that country changes. If we knew how to
chart it. People move, here to there. People are driven out. They
sort themselves differently. They camp on the outskirts of one
city while in another, neighborhoods are abandoned. People are
taken hostage, crippled, released, and after can't say by what
faction, though over here we say wars have sides. People leave
houses for sheds on slum rooftops, this isn't new, the papers
have told this story before. We hear the other rumors: the tell-
tale green-black skin, the cities we were told had been leafleted,
cleared of civilians. There everyone knows, they've all seen a
shovel tossed next to a dead man in a roadside ditch. To tell the
right story.

Every day it's new again. People go door to door to collect the stories, to determine scientifically at what rate death has
increased. They tally, record the means. Disease, bullet, bomb,
unknown. Unknown: no can say, one day, here, in a ditch, run
off the road. In a ditch, shot with his neighbors. In a ditch once
farmland, cratered by explosives. At least then there is a story,
something a family can carry. When the Americans first arrived

they found mass graves. This was satisfying, to prove this country had such secrets. Now it's a door kicked in, who is missing from that street, that jail cell, which market. No longer fields of the dead, severed from their names.

I was never in that country, never saw the faces and can't pronounce the names. I didn't stand with the doctors, staunching, stitching. I wouldn't know where to begin. But every day the war went on and so did I. We were secured, allied in survival. I was there to tally each day's deaths. I was there hungry for the newspaper. Every day the war resisted me, didn't include me. You will live on, it said, turning pictures toward me. Limbs in ice, a foot protruding, absurd. Soldiers' faces turned skyward. You will be fine.

# V

Late mornings I came downstairs, A at the door (is it that late? I always thought), my fatigue must have been visible. Those mornings, she knew me. Not the nights—I could be anyone when I'd gotten dressed, went out. But those mornings A walked in, always bringing something—wildflowers, fresh-baked bread, a book she'd finished—and kissed me on the cheek, Hello V, and put the kettle on.

(Her kiss usually low on the cheekbone, far back—how are there no more precise words for this landscape, where one place differs so much from another?—the fullness of flesh over the molars below the ridge of bone. But sometimes when coming or going she was careless or I turned; instead the kiss caught my ear, the earring, and her lips pressed the metal to me, warmed.)

You don't have to take care of me, I told A. You must have better things to do.

I should have said: I don't want to be indulged. But I am not elegant in the mornings; I blurt out; I take whatever's offered.

Someone making tea, making toast, making me a child. You don't have to do that, I said to A, but it was just one of those sentences, a gesture.

In the mornings when Z brought up anything—the news, what he and Ford had been planning, this or that article—I didn't respond. I resisted. I said something about the near-empty milk carton, the smell of the radiator in fall.

A knew better: she wanted to ask after my writing, but never did. How did you sleep? she asked. When I finally gave her a new manuscript, she ran her thumb along the edge of the pages. She thanked me. She told me small stories about her day.

Should I feel guilty that I don't remember what she said exactly? I remember how she pressed a mug to her face. I remember her listening, though that is a strange form of memory—to what? to me, it must have been—her expression, aware of me, of my words. Even what was commonplace, routine. This was just one of her gifts to me.

I did think of her as a writer; I thought of her as everything. Sister, daughter, caretaker, the one who answered the kettle, the one who endured—there aren't words for all these roles. For those who enter one's day only when it has fallen too silent. She fears I've always thought less of her. She tried to write whatever Ford wanted, whatever she described as (what did she say?) the most necessary, or was it urgent; she came to me, draft in hand, tearful or furious. But I didn't doubt her. In my memory her features are drawn in newsprint, impermanent, she belongs to this time, the present and all its voices; I creep back into silence. *The sentence*, I would lecture her, *should be a delicate arch*—but I should have reminded her, how anachronistic are arches, of amphitheaters, cathedrals, garden trellises: no use in the present. Its mirrored skyscrapers, its labyrinths of offices and prisons and rubble.

S

Z and I sat on the couch. One never thinks of him like that, at ease, sitting on the couch. I was just off work and had gone by A's, sat on the couch and shuffled the television forward. On television they were showing the four bodies, burned and swaying as they hung from the bridge, over the road, over the river. Is this true, would they have shown this? But I remember sitting there, the sun at an irritating angle, the window dirty where the dog pressed his nose to wait for A. The bodies blackened and moving in the wind.

Z was sitting next to me, leaning forward, elbows on his knees. The faces on the screen were shouting.

What did we see, what did we read about? A child's heel dug into the head of one of the men. His flesh already softened by fire. Someone had taken a piece of flesh, tied it to a stone, and flung it over a telephone wire. I should know, and I don't precisely, what happens in heat, the walls between blood vessels, skin, becoming—fat, liquefying? What remained on the sole of the shoe, on the fingers?

They tied the men to the backs of cars and dragged them through the streets to the bridge.

I expected Z to say something about what would come after. The siege we could already have predicted. But he didn't; we sat and watched. The bodies hung from the bridge at angles it was hard to understand. What was—that orange line, glowing, wrapped around a leg like a tendon unwinding? I hoped the bullets had killed them first or the smoke. That nothing of them could feel when the skin flaked back charred to expose the cavity of the stomach, the concavity the rib cage descends into, where the organs are held, then the hips. It seemed this place had fed itself fastest to fire, there was the least left here. Some of the faces around the bodies were smiling. A few men held up pieces of paper toward the camera, I never learned what they said.

When they stopped showing the pictures on one channel, you could flip to another and find them.

Goddammit, Z said, as the TV lost reception again. He hit the side of the TV and the dog raised his ears, a body moved again in a breeze.

It was strange to still call them bodies, they hung puppet-like and crackling, shedding as they were hoisted and moved. Children had run down the street toward the smoke. The day laborers, nothing to do, took out their shovels.

There was no electricity there, no water.

Z's phone buzzed on the table. I pushed it toward him. Vivienne. He hit the side, kept watching the screen. Didn't she go in for that test today? I asked. He nodded. But he didn't call back.

It's fine, I'll pick her up, he said later. It was becoming twilight. The dog had pressed his nose to the window and on-screen

the commentators had moved to the foreground, pictures behind them.

Z rubbed his hands along his face. We had turned the sound
off. Children's faces shone in the dust on the screen, laughing
or crying.

# A

A mosque, Z said.

A convenience store, F said.

I laughed, but they were serious.

You'd start a war with a mosque, F said.

I would point out the war we're already in, Z said.

I won't do it, I said. But they were looking only at each other.

In a convenience store, we could make s'mores over the fire, I said into the silence. Chocolate, marshmallows.

No one would understand, F said to Z.

I don't understand, I said.

# A

F led us into the heart of the city, train by train. The city breathed hot air down the stairs into each station, it was unbearable. Z passed his water bottle around and the middle-aged Quakers next to us shared their oranges and gave us peace buttons.

The stations were full of people coming for the march and locals fleeing it, we saw them standing with overnight bags on the opposite platform. High-school kids passed us shrilly, running up the stairs, wrists threaded through each other's elbows. There were college kids with signs and T-shirts, there were lawyers with earpieces and neon ball caps. We reached the sidewalk together. The city was sweating, the facades of the buildings thin in the heat and quivering. It felt as though mortar could soften, you could run a finger along the walls and the years would be a soft gritty cream you'd come away with. As we trudged our hair dampened and matted. Our clothes stuck to us and creased with our skin. We chanted. Our hands brushed each other's as we held up signs, sweat ran down forearms, we pushed things up through the crowd. A fake coffin, another. A parachute we fanned out around and grabbed. I could see the blood pulsing along F's temple: I watched it quicken as we moved forward.

This is right, I thought. We read all the time about the heat of that place. A desert land. But also: civilization had flowered there. We'd seen pictures of the date palms the army had plowed under. The livestock that in the aftermath wolves came for. So it couldn't have been quite the desert I imagined, thinking that day: this is right.

In the photographs the soldiers were wearing desert camo and outdated flak jackets and sweating. We were supposed to sympathize, to be outraged. But wouldn't refugees have driven, have walked in that heat, have waited six hours for gas, then faced the notorious roads? We'd read about the lines of men retreating across the desert years ago, how our soldiers had fired on them from above.

Sara was saying something: Dangerous, she said. Yes, we were vulnerable, gathered like this: I looked up.

On the news the next day there would be pictures of these streets, the crowds packed into them so closely that from above no pavement was visible. The sun flashed off the news helicopters.

I've always wondered: why do you see that white flash of tail whenever deer startle—a sign for the young to follow their mothers?

We didn't move forward: rumors came through the crowd that miles ahead the march had reached its destination. There was a festival in the park, people giving speeches. But we didn't see any of this.

F took my hand. We pushed through the crowd and out, slipped under the barriers. No cops here. We went down one alley and it turned into another. F stopped to piss down a grate. It looked as though people lived here: boxes, a sleeping bag, plastic bags filled and stacked, a smell. Where were they, we wondered— made to leave as the city had prepared itself, cleared its streets so we could fill them? It's not so bad, I said, looking around the alley, and F nodded. The light cut nicely across one corner, a cracked window shone. He kissed me. No one could see us. We didn't say anything, then said to each other—the crowd will still be there.

S

Of course I thought of going over there. I called programs and kept a notebook of the details. But it amounted to nothing. If you can't speak the language, they said. They said, the training there had been the best in the region, it's more a question of supplies, and they encouraged me to donate. But as the war went on, everyone admitted, the doctors and nurses were leaving, had left. Patients were left to piss in Pepsi bottles. You might be sent to three hospitals but not find a surgeon; finally someone would just amputate. And there were assassinations, even in hospitals. There didn't seem to be exceptions, as you might think; doctors were cleared from neighborhoods like anyone else. Like anyone else, their children ransomed; like anyone, a bullet in an envelope on the doorstep. But still it wasn't my place, still they didn't want me—it's not so simple, they said. Who thought it was?

I thought about stealing from the hospital where I'd trained, even from the shelter—everything was donated there, they could have replaced it all. No one even reads the invoices, I've seen their carelessness, piles of papers just flipped through. I could slip out antibiotics, needles, vaccinations. There must be a black-market price there for everything, I thought while in the supply room one day. For blood? I didn't know. I thought of those photographs, fire hoses trained on the streets to rinse them of blood.

These were the sort of photographs Z showed us, what was always up on his screen, he and Ford clicking through. Look, he said.

I could go there, I said once to Ford, I could nurse there. How much can it matter about the language? I have my hands.

They don't want you because you're an American, he said.

Ford was the only one I told these things and I shouldn't have. He never confided in me; it was all speeches with him, he never said one thing to me he couldn't have said to anyone.

So I'm here. All wars come to the shelter in time. The skin smoothes over the nub of an amputation.

My parents think this is noble work, but they don't want to hear about it. If they ask questions I sanitize my answers. There's no way to say how beneath my hands I can always feel the hair on the back where I press the stethoscope, the blood that browns around sutures.

I go to my parents' for dinner at least every two weeks. Over dinner they talk about the news as though it were something that happened to them and I couldn't know; they explain to me our own country.

I respond but don't argue. This is polite, but doesn't make me a good person.

I wash the dishes gloveless, unlike my mother.

But when I look at them I think they've changed, they're

older and anxious in ways I never saw as a child. My mother lets fruit rot in the basket; my father interrupts me too suddenly. It's their age, or the times.

I stay over because they don't like me to take the train back at night. To tell the truth I don't like it either, though I protest, though I always tell them it would be fine. I stay in my old room. They've left my textbooks on the shelves, two stuffed animals, the least ratty, poised beside them. From the window of my room I can see into the neighbors' upstairs, but in my whole life I've never seen anything of them I shouldn't have. There are photographs of me arranged around this room, but nothing recent, nothing after the graduation shot, backdrop of lilacs, and Ford, A, and I all trying not to squint in the sun.

In the morning I kiss my mother's cheek and even before breakfast it smells of Shalimar.

They don't know what other cities I've thought to live in, to leave for: there are whole years of me they don't know. This ignorance manifests as a quiet wariness. I too am wary, my hands never lingering too long on their furniture or silverware, the backs of their hands, a stranger's skin. We say goodbye in the kitchen, I kiss them both briefly. I know I cannot be free of them. They feel this too.

# F

I couldn't sleep at night because of the dog: I could hear him licking his paw, tongue across the same spot, over and over, breathing in through his nose. I think it went on for hours, I think it went on for years. Jesus fucking Christ—I cried out in the middle of the night. The dog settled for a moment, he exhaled. But by then A had woken up, pulled away from me to stare into the dark between us and the ceiling. She wouldn't go back to sleep.

What would it be like to have eleven thousand years of history? she said.

I don't know, I said. The sound of crickets. The dog's tongue again.

Air raid sirens and someone throwing open a door.

Summer rain, a rain of shrapnel, in the springtime in the ditches a rain of petals.

·

I saw a kid's hand once, Jay said, in a puddle. How does a bomb take just your hand?

What happened to it?

I don't know, Jay said, the kid died.

Just from missing a hand?

I think from missing all the blood.

.

Jay said: The nights were too loud there, people started sleeping during the day. We'd go to do our raids or whatever and we'd be waking them up in the middle of the day, the whole family, that seemed like the rudest thing.

.

Is it true you hear the bombers beforehand, like a whisper? I asked him.

I don't know.

.

What were we eleven thousand years ago? A asked. People, I mean.

The same, I said. Just shorter. And lived less time. Fewer teeth.

.

Short sirens meant the beginning of the attack, a long one meant it had ended.

·

Once I was out in the lot behind the high school and found Jay with his friends, laughing, spray paint cans scattered. *You suck PRs*, the wall read. Puerto Ricans—I had to ask him.

·

I wanted the faces at the checkpoints. What they found searching people's drawers.

Jay didn't talk about any of this.

I heard him practice guitar through the wall, the same chords over and over. Jesus Christ, can't you just learn Stairway, I asked him.

He didn't answer.

·

Lunch, I'd say up the stairs. All it meant was that I'd made a sandwich. He didn't come down. I could have gone up and knocked. But later there'd be more bread missing.

·

The family of a man in Jay's unit was getting deported and he wanted to write a letter in protest. Will you read this? Jay asked me. He kept trying to put in these stories. In the end I just wrote it for him.

I never found out what happened with the family. At Jay's funeral I asked the guy but it was all still in process.

They say the saint had whispered, Bury me in the first place the camel kneels.

·

I can't fucking stand it, A said in the morning. If you wake me up one more time.

The dog keeps me up, I said, and I tried to explain.

So sleep on the couch, she said.

Why can't I kick the dog out?

No, she said, it's not like that. You sleep on the couch.

Dogs are scavengers, I said. If you saw him eating a body on the street, you'd feel differently.

But I don't see that, she said.

She said: I tell him not to pee in the neighbor's garden, I do that.

You love that dog too much, I told her, protecting her pointlessly.

It's natural, she said. It's human.

You don't even know what you mean by that, I said.

# S

Z was pacing A's kitchen, the smell of mint strong through the windows. A had let mint take a whole corner of the yard. We had mint tea, tabbouleh, whatever she thought of.

A church, Z said.

Jesus Christ, Viv said, Are we the KKK?

It would be empty, he said, we'd do almost no damage. Just something on the altar, maybe.

Where they keep the wine and the wafers, Viv said. Our natural enemies.

A was just looking at Z, curious.

Do you have a particular church in mind? Ford said.

No, Z said, That doesn't matter.

After a pause Z said, Isn't it the point, that all the wine, all the bread is one body?

Yes, A said.

I can't tell how serious this is, I said. Is this a theological discussion or are we—

Oh, let's label the conversation so Sara knows where to file it, Vivienne said, reaching for the wine Ford was pushing toward her.

Well, would you do it? I asked her.

Do what? Viv said.

Bomb a church.

What matters is what it would say, she said, not whether I'd say it.

That's nice philosophy, I said, but—

Then file it under philosophy, she said, What a relief that must be for you.

No one said anything.

You could also call it a metaphor, Viv said, now that I think about it.

It's not the worst idea, Ford said.

Z was at his computer screen, no longer listening.

# V

Z didn't like to visit his parents, but we'd go. I went with him, though I didn't ask him to do the same, slipped off by myself to my own hometown. But I liked watching him fight his mother to do the dishes; I liked watching him sit stiffly in their living room. You too are human, I thought. His mother coming and going from the kitchen, refilling plates of crackers and carafes well before they emptied. His mother's hands in passing swept over the top of Z's head, curved round a shoulder, as though remembering the child loose-skinned and yowling, sunburned and too thin, the years between that body and this gone at her touch. Z didn't pull away.

Your hair's thinning, she said to him once, and laughed.

I know, he said.

Oh dear, I was just kidding, she said.

I looked at him—it was true, the hairline shell-shaped around the widow's peak; I hadn't noticed.

From your mother's side, his father said, the genes. Don't blame me.

Z's father was a doctor, a decade retired. He spoke with his hands officiously fingertip to fingertip, though the knuckles of the fingers had thickened, the arch strained. And that's what my hands will look like, I thought, noting how rarely he got up, how his wife pushed things closer to him on the table.

Z's father watched me, as though hunting out illness. He would have liked to test me, I thought, as he caught me staring off, it would have seemed to him at nothing, though out the window there had been a cardinal, the first that spring. He would have liked the whole clinical workup: run a fork along the bottom of the feet, the toes nodding, give all the commands: *Who is the vice president? Count backward from one hundred by sevens. Close your eyes.*

He didn't approve of my drinking, so we always brought the wine.

They would ask Z something about his magazine, something general that they wouldn't have to have read it to ask; the conversation would turn to politics. Z didn't bring it up; it was always one of them. Z's mother had been in Chicago in '68 during the convention and this story always worked its way in. Z's father bailing her out. The first few times it had been a good story, easy to picture, her in overalls, a cabled sweater, thick hair slipping from its braid as it did now.

I got up before she could and added cheese to the cheese plate.

My novel sat on the coffee table; I had signed the front flyleaf for them, *With love always.*

Sometimes they would say of Z's magazine, *That was an excellent article,* or *I'm not sure about...*

Z argued with his parents, he never held back, though I tried to stop him, to offer something light, a distraction. Or else to prove my appeal I would side against him—because it should all have been a game: his father's irrefutable fingers, his mother breaking in with some snipe at the president, or to tell how she saw that famous actor once, too, at another protest, what they had said to each other. I would try to say this or that, about how everything was different now, only to be disagreed with by everyone. Which I'd hoped would resolve things—unite them in opposition—but it rarely did.

We could use that money at home, his father said, meaning the war.

Z hadn't been disagreeing with this, but now the conversation proceeded as though he had. Z started to respond, to talk of transitions and reparations, but his father waved a hand and, following it, the evening returned to its accustomed stiffness. Someone announced some opinion. In the dusk of the room there was no real answer, and I watched the low light pierce the wine, with my wrist I tilted the glass through a slow revolution. If the sky were always this color, I said, how would we live? Everyone looked at me or away, and Z's mother said, It's past time for dinner. She rose to gather the plates. I followed her to the kitchen, wrapped the ends of each cheese.

·

When I visit them now, I see my novels in the corner of the living-room bookshelf, tucked in next to Dickens. They ask me about them, tell me when they've read a review. Don't worry about that woman in the *Times*, Z's mother says, She's an idiot, I never agree with her.

I know I should feel this as kindness.

She'll mention some article, the latest election, and say:

Now, I wonder what he would have thought about that.

I wonder, I say.

There are these pauses.

You have swallows in your eaves, I say, pointing to the window, the bush where they're darting.

I know, Z's father says. We're supposed to have them taken care of, but we can't bring ourselves—

They turn their heads toward the window, then back toward me; the birds chatter.

# F

I told her the true story but she laughed, she didn't believe me.

We'd had a class together. We sat near each other and laughed together at nothing. There was nothing funny about the class, a history of the Middle East, popular that semester. At first I sat behind A. When there was nothing to take notes about she gathered her hair up off her neck for no reason, her elbows winged. She didn't tie it up, just let it fall back. I watched her and after a week sat next to her.

We weren't drunk, maybe it was almost dinnertime. We walked past the campus clichés, the stone chapel, the new concrete wheelchair ramp. We were talking about class then we weren't. We were joking about places we'd never been. Wait, are you religious? she asked me, stopping herself.

We went to my room. For a book, we said. Then we were in bed, clothes still half on. My stubble chafed her, though I was the one who saw this and said something. She didn't care, pressed herself back to me.

I didn't know her name. Really. I knew I should have but I didn't. I knew her neck sloping up, hair through her fingers.

A, I said. Because this was the first letter, I was sure of that.

She laughed maybe, but she didn't mind. She called me F, which I liked.

A, I thought.

She was telling me about a rally on campus that weekend. You should come—she was saying, fingers light on my collarbone—Even if it's small, it's something, right?

I heard about it, sure, I said. I'll be there.

A beginning.

# A

What do I even remember of the years in school? I would go to visit F in his lab. I would hold the mice in my hand. Their nails scratched at my palm and I imagined his days, lifting them from the cage, their feet tickling his heart line.

It's not just that memory begins in childhood, but that we learn to make memories as children. Later we can't alter those molds, only add to the series. I believe this. I still feel the daddy longlegs on my ankle as a child. I kicked it off and cried out. I smelled wild grapes, I smelled lavender, the well-kept gardens mingling. I clipped the chives and my brother and I folded them up in our mouths and chewed, onion and dirt, then breathed on each other. We ate the sweet clover we found in the fields. Filled jars with fireflies.

Snow was the cold's answer to fireflies, I thought later. In the winter F and I walked out into the fields to smoke. The path had disappeared and we tromped our own way, snow slipping beneath the tongues of our shoes. In the twilight the snow was pricks of cold light on our faces, in our eyelashes. We stopped and smoked by the red pines, which had been planted together and were all the same height. When we were high enough we made snow angels, the snow not deep enough, so my back-bone rubbed roots I couldn't see. The seat of F's pants was stiff with ice when we got back, the denim holding its own made-up form. I laughed at it, we laughed.

In the morning the fields were crusted over with light, and I wished that we had never gone out. Our footprints ruined what would have stretched unbroken, past the tennis courts, to the trees. Our path marring what would have been wildness.

Wildness—what we all hunted for as children, among the beds of dead needles, rocks we hid from each other behind, the mud of the streambeds and the moss we'd take turns lying in, looking out for spiders. We were never far from home then, from the street where shrubs crept in demurely. We longed to get lost but even when we pushed each other farther into the woods, when we challenged one another, it was a game, a show. We would never starve to death there, no matter what we said. We would never have to eat squirrels, berries, mushrooms. The squirrels ran from us anyway, we couldn't tell good berries from bad, we knew nothing about mushrooms except to stomp on the puffballs.

F and I had walked out, the snow blowing; it was hard to see but we trekked forward. We laughed at ourselves, at our cold hands as we tried to light the joint and snowflake after snowflake stiffened our knuckles, extinguished the flame. Then we lit it and this was a victory. When we got back inside, we stood stripped to our underwear in the bathroom, running hot water over our hands, we laughed. His curls were wet where snowflakes had been, and in the mirror I saw the shallow valleys between his ribs, the ridges of bone in the fluorescence, the thin living skin.

# F

The daffodils were up after Jay died. Dad insisted on cutting the tree down and he dragged the limbs of it through the daffodils. He dragged the limbs into the swamp behind the house, to where we couldn't see them. He'd have the stump out too, he said. But that would take some equipment, which Mom didn't want in the yard, not before she'd hosted the reception.

People ate egg salad off paper plates and spoke quietly. Everyone looked older, these parents, than I remembered. The kids from the neighborhood came in ties and didn't joke about anything. It was hot for jackets and I took mine off. I sat on the stump to drink and no one spoke to me there.

After Jay died my parents started going to meetings. Middle-aged hippies wearing too many scarves came by our house. My parents stood with them on street corners and held signs, they stood on the corner by the convenience store. They marched on town hall by the dozen slowly. My parents didn't know the songs. They started talking about the war and mispronounced everything.

Later tiger lilies bloomed in the ditches by the roadside. You could find dead deer among them, hauled over, swollen.

People wanted to interview us. I tried to talk at a meeting once, college students soft-eyed before me, but halfway through I had nothing to say.

I moved out.

I didn't go to grief counselors. I didn't talk to other families.

In the paper the bodies piled up. The numbers ticked up. Missiles, precision-guided, landed in the wrong places. The photos of hospitals showed dirty bandages on dirty floors.

Are we redeemed?

This was my question.

When Jay died I became closer to the war, closer to the knowledge I wanted. I knew what loss was then. I used him for this. I believe he wanted this for me.

He didn't leave a note and I wish he had. I don't remember our conversations exactly, just the idea of them, I don't remember what words he chose. I don't remember the feel of him, though his hand was sometimes on my shoulder, though we slept with only a wall between us.

Every country has its dead and that country is no different. In the graves, heads nestle next to one another, hands not touching. His silence is no less foreign to me. I would rather have laid his body in some field with theirs. No one would have noticed one more loss in that country. I would have added his bones to theirs and so I too would have joined them, bound myself to them.

We would do anything to bring him back, my parents say, in the interviews, in the living-room meetings, in crowded college halls. You don't know anything anymore, I want to tell them.

# A

The child had been taken while gathering coins in the street with his father. I read this three times, but I always pictured it wrong. I pictured the child standing in a fountain lined with coins, gathering. The fountain would be dry. But I didn't even know if there were fountains in that country, if this was a way to make wishes there.

I read: the family paid the ransom but the child was not returned.

Here, I kept getting phone calls: People wanted to dam the river nearby and build a power station. This had been in the works for some time. *Come support us,* they said on the phone, and told me when the meetings were. *We have to reduce our dependence on…* they began to explain. I know, I said, I understand that. In the mail I got leaflets from protestors, groups opposing the dam. The leaflets had photographs of fish and plants that might be adversely affected. The fish looked dead already, blurred in black-and-white, blank-eyed. The plants looked like weeds that grab at the ankles and slime on the river bottom when you get in to swim.

All of us neighborhood kids had swum in that river. A bend in it where it pooled, where there were warm rocks to lie on, an incline where you could lie and let the water drag sticks and leaves under you. Together at night we picked our way toward the swimming hole, we thought we could find it by sound, *that's the bend*, someone would say and the rest follow. They might be right. We always got there. Wearing sneakers to protect us from the broken bottles. But the glass might still press up into us as we lay in the dark on the rock faces coupling, uncomfortable, the sound of the water never as loud as we wanted, never drowning us out as we wanted.

In the daylight we would jump from a small cliff on the side. Someone had put up a rope swing, but you had to throw yourself forward just right or you'd hit a rock shelf below. One boy had hit it, paraplegic. In the daylight he should have seen: the water was too golden there. Some people said his neck hadn't broken till after, when the other kids pulled him from the water.

I hadn't been there since I was a kid. F and I had gone to a protest against the dam, years ago. We didn't know anything about it, but someone had called us and we went. We'd sat in the yard of the power company offices and held signs. It was hot out and there were only a dozen people there, probably the same pamphlets, the same plants and fish. We'd brought a bag of cherries; I remember spitting pits into the grass.

Whenever I think of the dam I picture it wrong; I picture the water itself electrified. The blade of the waterfall descending to shock the pool below. The bodies of the teenagers who swam there would rise to the surface, bellies translucent and bloating. The water lilies brightening as the current passed through them, stinging any fingertips that touched them.

This is not how it is.

They explained on the phone how many households the station could power.

I read that the mother would stand for hours holding a photograph of the child and crying. The family would come home to find her like this. They wanted to hide the photograph, but she had to take it to the offices and morgues once a week.

They say there are places in that country where oil rises if you just press your thumb to the ground.

*It would be a waste not to*, they say to me on the phone. A waste of a river. I wonder. Waste, how you lose a coin on the street and the coin loses a child. How plant and animal carcasses pool under rock underground. We swam in that summer-low river. We pictured workmen unearthing the cherry trees we left in that lawn. Our bodies curved out so gracefully in descending to the water, rising back to the surface, wasting the rock shelf that might have touched the spine, coaxed the bones into falling just wrong.

S

The woman next to me on the bus got up from her seat and pushed past. My bag rustled and the pink writing on the box of the pregnancy test was legible through the plastic. I looked around—who had seen it? That old man, that teen-aged girl? I pushed the bag back behind my calves. I thought, well, the body answers to none of us. And for all they know I could be trying, I'm not so young anymore that people assume disaster.

Disaster? A lover's finger below my ear, the line of bone there vertical and beside it a soft place, just finger-shaped, I hadn't realized. Though I had checked pulses, felt glands so near to it. He touched me there, then folded his hand back, put his knuckles underneath my chin, more predictably. But these things don't always have to be new.

Now: one hand holds the bag with the test in it, another the bus grip. It's probably nothing; I work too many twelve-hour shifts and am overtired. The body is unreliable. My hand even fumbled at an IV the other day; I had been up too late, with him—embarrassing.

And if yes, what? Imagine the possible futures, the palm across the lower belly and the ache in the breasts nourishment, not desire. I picture—it's this vague; I don't even think boy or girl—the *child*, a toddler, in front of me where the path widens on the way to the stream behind A's. Tire tracks, fox prints, rabbits, deer: the child, my child, among them. This isn't possible: I don't live there anymore, we don't go to that place together, that's past. But I like this thought, the hawks minding that clearing, the sun widening overhead, Z throwing a stick for the dog, who never played with sticks. The child's feet in that stream, small and right.

It's unforgivable, really—thinking to raise children in the past, it makes me no better than anyone, no better than—well. Who wouldn't wish, perversely, to have a child even in the midst of true disaster, just to say, there is more, something not only endures but grows, day by day, becomes someone separate enough to lose. How my parents are satisfied chiding me about my politics: they wish they could get as far from themselves.

What would anyone feel at the sound of the planes? We can picture it, mother clutching child; we can even see, in those few terrible places where the blast was hot and fast enough, the true shape of a family: the silhouette of skin seared onto wall. There is a building like this in Baghdad, now a memorial to that bombing. When I think of these things, all I can imagine is to be the child, clutching—the children we read about, discovered afterward surviving days in the demolished houses. What a mother feels I don't know.

I think of this when hands run along me—a waste, I want to say, his mouth at my breast. The night, the story proceeds. So why not, finally, something unexpected, new? A child walking through the past along the deer trails, of no interest to hawks, in the sun? Why not, when so many surprises are no more than: planes breaking through the heat and dark, downstairs the children bored and crying, a siege that goes on so long the dead must be buried in the garden.

Why not, I bend toward his touch or any, the back arches, unthinking.

The test's negative. Fine.

# F

I don't go on dates, I can't stand it. *What do you do? Where are you from?* I've tried but I just jiggle the drink in my hand and make people nervous. I know this because one woman put her hand over mine and said, You're making me nervous.

If you just go to bars, things can work out better. I'm better. You sit not facing each other, but facing the rows of bottles, the taps, the mirror, whatever it is. There are TVs to pretend to look at, ball games and cheering that rises up and drowns out whatever you were saying, she was saying, you can keep using that moment if you need it, start talking about something else.

.

I'm a lawyer, the blond next to me had said. Then: I know, I look young—this must have been in response to whatever look I'd given her. She drank from a red cocktail straw that kept getting caught in the lime wedge and I couldn't decide if I was interested.

We'd been talking about torture memos. I hadn't brought it up. Fucking unbelievable, she'd said, but swearing didn't come naturally to her. I listened. And he's still a judge, she said: I mean, we're trying to impeach him.

Who's we, I wondered.

She knew a lot. She knew names of laws I didn't know, she had the series of events down precisely. You can't have much luck with this line, I thought, looking around the bar—she had been talking for ten minutes maybe, saying: They'd put him in a box, like the size of a coffin, and leave him there. Even they had to stop doing that because there was no way it was legal. They pretended to put scorpions in, she said, but it was just to scare him, really they were caterpillars.

There was a replay on the TV screen, the bar cheered. We both looked up. A player was trotting around the bases. Nice, she said.

I leaned in, I kissed her. A little hard. She didn't do anything, but she didn't move away. I could tell she didn't like my hand half on her leg, half on the stool, pulling her in.

Well, she said, but didn't say anything else.

All that talk of interrogation techniques, I said.

I'm kidding, I said.

Words had been scrolling across the bottom of the TV the whole time, stock quotes, headlines. A body count from the drone that had bombed a village in the mountains earlier that day, I'd been reading about it before I came here, maybe she had too.

I nodded up at the headline. Unmanned, I said, the way of the future. Soon we'll be nostalgic for the days when people had to kill people themselves.

That's not funny, she said. She had moved her head between me and the screen, a little unsteadily.

I know, I said.

# A

F calls me every few weeks. I think he's always stoned when he does this.

I've been having dreams, he says.

This isn't enough to reply to, so I wait.

I dream about finding Z's body, he says.

On the other end of the phone I picture a rock rolled back from the mouth of a tomb. Nonsense.

It's his hand, F says, it's Z's hand, how in the photo it was reaching out.

It wasn't reaching, I say to him—I think I say it kindly. He was dead so it wasn't reaching.

Clutching, F says, the fingers curved just like that.

I can't see him but I think he's gesturing to show me.

·

I dream that this city is under siege, he says.

I don't know what this means.

It isn't like a bombing, he says, it's a feeling. A tightening. A circling in. The light goes, then the power, then the air.

That's the sort of dream you have before you wake up to find your face is in the pillow, I say, you've turned over and it's hard to breathe.

No, I feel it around my neck, suffocating me.

Then—I pause—maybe whoever's next to you has thrown an arm…?

No, he says.


•


The night before he died Z walked with us down to the stream. He said: Even at night, the sky here doesn't darken. The trees are black against the light even in what should be darkness. What's called darkness. The sky is the purple of a day-old bruise, Sara said. V nodded.


•


For most of the siege there was a blackout. It was hard to know for how long because after a while the blackout, having become routine, was no longer mentioned. There were only car headlights. Oil fires, blackening further out. Bombs.


•


When I think of Z's hands, I think of him at his laptop, thumb loud on the space bar, shoulders hunched and face thrust toward the screen. Your back, I say, you'll hurt yourself—the sort of thing Sara would say. V sweeps a hand sleepily through Z's hair. Are you having another, I say to F at the fridge and he doesn't reply.

It might be close to dawn. There might be Xs of duct tape across all the windows. I run a finger along each line of an X, leaving fingerprints to blur the glass.

Good night, Sara says as she goes.

# A

What, are you going on a date? F asked my reflection. He had been up all night and had come to bed just a few hours before. The mirror was still foggy from the shower and I wiped a circle clean.

What are you doing up? I asked.

I have to pee, he said, and pushed past me.

I have to go see my professor, I said, over the sound of him pissing. But his eyes were half-closed, he was almost asleep.

You look like you're going to a cocktail party, he said. It's like nine in the morning.

I didn't look at him, just finished with the eye shadow.

I fucked up, I said, I missed a whole exam in that research methods class, I said to his back as he reached for the towel. He shrugged or maybe just dried his hands.

•

My professor—who had made his name reporting on the nuclear age, the dangers of waste and dissemination—smelled like scrambled eggs and offered me coffee. He didn't ask but put creamer in it, vanilla and disgusting. I should drink it, I thought, these are the sort of things that can matter to people. I sipped. I sat upright.

So what are we going to do about your exam? he asked me.

I'm really sorry, I said, then stopped.

I would assume so, he said. But you can't get graduate credit for regret.

I almost said, Yes, sir, but changed it at the last minute to: Of course not, I understand.

I hated his hand tapping flat-palmed on his desk.

It's not only the exam, he said. Your last assignment was more or less a mess, as I mentioned at the time.

Yes, I said. I'd written the whole thing one night on the couch, F and Z downstairs at their makeshift workbench, the dog trotting between us. I wrote about that march, but I didn't do any background, and I didn't interview F, Z, Sara, or Viv, just used things I thought they had said. This had its own logic, which no one would question if I pulled it off—I'm sure I stole this rationale from F.

Yes? he said, Does that mean you can do better?

Yes, I can, I said. He had a fireplace in his office. In a framed photo he shook hands with the director of the IAEA and everyone smiled.

You don't sound that confident, he said.

What if I asked him: A recruiting center, a post office?

He might have agreed with me on the post office: this we could have discussed.

Do you ever regret—I started to say this out loud. I meant

the office, I meant the whole thing, the tweed jacket with patches on the elbows he almost had.

He raised his eyebrows: Do I regret what?

Nothing, I said. I said, Sometimes I get distracted.

Well, it's time to be serious, he said, tapping the desk once with his palm. You can't keep doing things by halves. That's not what you're here for.

There was a pause.

Did you just *forget?* he asked me.

Sort of, I said. No, not exactly.

He waited for me to say more, but I didn't. He looked at me: Well, we'll do the makeup next Thursday, then. Two o'clock.

I nodded.

You're capable of good work, he said, Better work.

You don't sound that confident, I said, looking over his shoulder at his perfect bookshelves.

He looked surprised.

I said, Sorry. See you next Thursday. Thanks.

I walked down the hallway trying to remember where the books for that unit were. Under the bed, on the windowsill? I remembered V tucking the worst one under her arm to take to the bathroom, a joke. Had I seen it since then? She couldn't be trusted not to hide it among the towels for no reason. Oh God, I thought—maybe F knows. He wouldn't help, though, he would just laugh at me, from the bed run his hand down my leg as I kneeled to look beneath, swept my hand through the dog hair and stray socks, looking for it by shape, my hand brushing that bottle.

# F

It surprised me, when Z began asking more questions, offering ideas for actions, targets. What about—he'd say, and he'd have a list. Soon there were handfuls of lists, all his.

Come have a look at this, he'd say, gesturing at his laptop. His magazine was doing a series on PTSD and vets, interviews and stories of domestic abuse or suicide; he kept wanting me to get involved. He asked me to write something, and when I didn't, he asked A.

I came over to look, but he kept editing as I read, scrolling up and down, it was impossible. I didn't say much. Did this disappoint him? He'd just nod, thumb hitting the space bar.

I used to ask him, Have you eaten? This is how much Vivienne had gotten to me, that I'd be sure to ask him if he wanted a sandwich.

You drink, then go back to work? he asked me at one of our lunches.

Sure, I said.

He raised an eyebrow.

We kill all the animals anyway, I said, which wasn't quite true.

Z came to my old lab once, curious, he said. He held a mouse in his hand and asked me what we were planning to do with it. Nothing, I said, that one's a control.

Lucky bastard, he said and smiled, put it back in its cage.

My hand did slip once, the needle went not into the brain but deep into the belly. There's nothing to do in those cases but finish them off, which I did, and flipped the gloves inside out.

Z criticized my map of that country, how I noted each soldier's death with a dot, to see when the dots would blanket the map. What about the people there, he said, isn't that the point. The civilians.

There's no way to, I said.

What about—and I knew he was going to ask about Jay.

·

Once, not long after Jay died, we were out and Z lifted my beer away from me, handed me a water.

He's an older brother, Vivienne said as he walked away. She meant to whisper, but she was loud, she too was always drunker than anyone wanted. It was hard to tell how she did it, it seemed as if she always had the same glass in her hand.

She rumpled my hair, which didn't come naturally to her, her fingers pausing curiously on the scalp.

I don't mean that he understands, she said. Just that's why he's like that.

I'm an only child, she stated after a pause. Think of all the things I don't know.

·

I could have told her:

Jay's hair clippings littered over the sink. His jacket smelled like some girl, like weed, like cherry air freshener. The phone ringing, but it's not for you. His girlfriend came over, you could hear her pressed up against his door right away. You did better than him in every class and you mentioned it at dinner, said things loudly in the kitchen about honors chem—he came home once with a propane burner line along his thumb, red and tender, he couldn't play basketball for a week. There was a condom wrapper between the car seats. He didn't say anything about the month you spent helping the guys start a meth lab in a trailer out by the tracks. You must have stunk of it, but he never asked. Once he gave you a ride home when you couldn't get your hands to sit right on the steering wheel and called. He had a friend over and they were playing action figures in the basement and invited you down. When you played soccer in the backyard he'd get the ball when you kicked it out, even down by the property line, where the grass was soaked in mud so that when he kicked mud sprayed over him. He gave you copies of his old tests but you didn't use them. You didn't even have to ask, he'd lie to your parents every time about when he'd heard you come in. At the end you gave him ride after ride. You let him throw up whenever, your car smelled lemon and sweet, Lysol and stomach acid. The two of you had the same shoulder blades, too much like wings—A ran her finger along yours laughing—jerseys looked stupid on both of you. You held his shoulders outside the bar, he didn't have anything to throw up anymore, but he was trying to keep your car clean.

In the rearview you could see his chin clean-shaven, pressed against the cool of the window to keep his head steady, his eyes flicking at passing cars, lights blurring toward him, he didn't pass out. When you looked back at him in the rearview his eyes were always open.

# A

Is it love, this old surprise? To note who the face across from me isn't. At a coffee shop, in bed: not F. The hand is not the same and pauses on the stomach, not the hip as I was used to, but I turn. In the morning across from me drinking coffee is not F but—this man, he's a journalist, he takes cream and sugar, he smiles as we make love, all this is new, every time.

We met in Arabic class. He had covered the war, lived over there for a year: this is how we started talking. He had ridden down the roads, through the neighborhoods I'd read of, had ridden aid convoys in after the siege. He had seen the slums from a Humvee, the sewage down the street and above it rows of posters of clerics. We talked and talked. After class, at the coffee shop, without meaning to I was leaning forward, the metal table gridding my forearm. He had no trouble telling the stories. He used the same phrases as in his articles, I looked them up later. He wore sunglasses and I couldn't see his eyes.

Are you a student here? he'd asked, waving his hand at the brick building now behind us.

Oh no, I said, just the one class. I used to be in grad school, a few years ago, somewhere else—I started saying, but didn't finish. I didn't want to tell him it was his vocation I had failed at, shrugged off.

I must have seemed well-meaning and useless to him: one of those women who works in development for some NGO, joins listservs, learns snippets of languages she'll never use. This class, what could it give me? *Thank you for the tea. Which way to the market?*

A convoy ahead of him had hit an IED, he told me later. He'd seen one soldier flung out in the road, his leg gone and more blood, he said, than you could imagine.

A strange phrase, I thought, when I could only imagine any of it, the whole scene, the whole country, and it wasn't any harder, to picture a ditch filled with blood.

What happened to him? I asked. But he didn't know. Sent home probably, he said, to get fixed up. You wouldn't believe how they're patching guys up—he paused and sipped from his beer—The medicine's so good they survive anything now, but sometimes when you see these guys you wonder if that's really better.

Sometimes, I said.

When we made love he didn't stop smiling.

I hated it.

I feel safe here, he said, pulling me toward him, the pillows folding awkwardly beneath. For once I'd like to be the stronger one, the one who pulls, who can't just be shifted in sleep by any set of hands.

His looks were right for that country, which helped him there, though he didn't speak the language. One of the first times we met he explained: That's why I'm in the class, it's always bothered me that I can't speak the language of my grandparents.

We went through the workbooks, practiced dialogues together. This was the nicest part: fingers following the words together backward.

We sat next to each other in class. So little changes, I thought.

Were you never tempted, I wanted to ask, to slip out of the Humvee into the streets? You could pass there, couldn't you?—I wasn't sure—you could have gone off anywhere and seen everything.

And been kidnapped as soon as I opened my mouth, he could have replied. We'd all seen the videos.

But this was how things were there: it would at least have been a true story.

When we made love he still smiled.

For once, I thought—the same contentment crinkled around his eyes—for once swear, cry, throw up, anything.

He loved me, he said in the dark once as I was almost sleeping.

·

F wouldn't say anything, he'd come over to my desk and take my pen, put it down, pull me over. I wouldn't quite protest. We didn't speak, what did we have left to say to each other? Sometimes he smiled.

·

I didn't care for the journalist's articles, not really. If I had known him better, if he had asked me, I'd have taken a red pen to them. But why would he ask me, of all people? My expertise in grant-writing?

But what a story, I thought sometimes, if I told him everything he would have said: Jesus Christ, what a story. He might remember Z's name, which had lingered in the news longer than we'd expected. Then again, he might not say that—he might just listen, stroke my hair. If it were such a scoop, wouldn't I have written it? Wouldn't—it's not impossible; we all could imagine it—have Z?

# V

I consider the genres: Interview. Manifesto. Lede.

Love letter.

Flower on gravestone.

Flowers on gravestones—which somehow never rot in the cemetery I walk through daily, I've noticed this, the petals never damp and stinking; someone must come by to neaten up.

Lede. The other day I went to a fund-raiser, with speeches, a group that builds schools over there, that brings—really—packets of pencils, notebooks, and prosthetic limbs. Workbooks in two languages, theirs, ours. A had called me and told me to go; a journalist friend of hers was speaking about his two trips to the war, unembedded. He was good-looking, that I acknowledged. He talked passionately about *the people*. You can't write a love letter to a whole people, I ought to have said to him. My chair was hard and uncomfortable. I did say something to him afterward: I shook hands with him, his warm soft palms—you shouldn't be so vague, I said, which was a blow, I could see that in his eyes.

But I was right.

But he has been places I haven't. He has seen the streets after the soldiers left, the checkpoints absent and children setting up stands on the corners, handing out juice to passing cars.

But this is not the stuff of love letters either; this is what I mean to clarify. Nor when the women in front of the cameras wail—that's the only word for it—and beat their chests, crying the names of children, husbands, brothers, lost. This is something else. Just as I do not write for Z, or to him or anyone.

I clapped politely at the journalist's speech.

The clapping like the click of a shutter. The journalist had clicked through a slideshow of photographs, including a series from a morgue: It was so terrible, he said, I took pictures mechanically. The bodies weren't whole; limbs piled up. They could no longer assemble them as bodies, but leg, leg, arm, arm. There were, terribly, heads. One watched the photos click by, the clicking not quite as soft as hands clapping, not the same. But how did they know, that this leg, for instance, didn't belong with this arm? This head this hand? Perhaps no one had looked closely enough, to see how this wrist bone might resemble that ankle. How this sock might match fingers that could have pulled on it, old habit, a child's thin calves.

I should have raised my hand to say: There's nothing mechanical to it. Only human.

What do you know? the journalist should have answered me.

And how vague it must feel, and impossible, to try to bring back a whole country. Even the easiest moments, the greetings and muttering the interpreters talked over, the tea one was offered, the aid packages stacked in truck beds and argued through checkpoints. He said people there kept asking the same questions of anyone who talked to them, the most urgent questions.

Cameras documented this or that explosion but were absent the hours a family sat by their window watching the sniper watch the street. The dogs and cats in the street. Sometimes the sniper shot the dogs. Out of boredom or dedication or—it could be, there was no way to know otherwise—so that the bodies still on the streets would not be further desecrated (if that's what dogs did, or one could call it natural) before their families could come for them.

It was the journalist who told me about the dogs; I learned this from him.

Thank you, I said after the speech, and shook his hand. Thinking as I did that his hand had held A. But he could never claim he knew her better than I did; differently, but never better.

·

Love letters: this thought isn't mine, was born in an interview. When I read your novels, the interviewer said, they seem to me to be *love letters*. She didn't say to Z, but that's what she meant, I was sure. I didn't answer at first; I'm never sure what to say when people say these things. What do they think of him, now that even the war is old news. She and I waited for each other.

That's interesting, I finally said, realizing that it must be more my turn than hers.

Have you ever thought of your writing this way?

No, I said, which wasn't quite true; I had thought: one cannot write for the dead. I thought she'd take my denial as a compliment, but instead she tipped her head sideways and waited.

One cannot write for the dead, I said. Is this sincerity, I wondered.

But wouldn't you say people write for the dead all the time? That that's exactly what they're trying to do?

But failing, I said.

All right, trying but failing.

All right, I said, We agree, but I don't think this is what I am failing at.

She waited.

You see, I didn't write to him when he was alive.

Write to him?

She hadn't been thinking of Z, then. Zechariah, I said, I'm sorry, Zechariah Berkman, isn't that who we were talking about? You know the story?

I didn't mean—her eyes widened; I waved a hand.

Never mind, I said. But one can't write a love letter generally, one always writes *to*, you know.

But—

It's like soldiers' letters home, they're only interesting if you imagine who loosens the flap with a finger and thinks of how he sealed it. The letters themselves are nothing.

Or: the journalists, I said. They don't file these reports, bombings in the background, thinking of *people*. There's someone they think of when they wire their latest. That's how it works. One doesn't go down into the morgue the day after the siege for no one. One looks at the bodies and thinks who they might be. How much hands are like hands. How similarly all our skin holds. Then writes.

Her job of course was to take notes, not to have a conversation. I watched her type.

•

Ford and I already did it, Sara had said to me the night Z died—she had come to get me, I must have been sitting on the kitchen floor for hours. The refrigerator was too loud and cars kept going by. We went to identify him, she said, You don't need to go. It was hard, she added, which I understood to mean the state he was in.

We should go to A's, she said, and slipped her hand around my elbow, hard, to pull. I wasn't sure why this should be next, but I followed her.

By then it was nearly morning. How lucky that I wasn't in that country, where had an explosion claimed him I couldn't have just sat where I learned of it, just sat. The planes above still coming, or the sirens rushing toward. It was not like that here; no one would worry that they'd look for a body, check everywhere thinkable, and find no one, nothing. Limbs they'd have to sort through to see, and even then, bury what? A left arm? And the death squads buried their victims everywhere, they don't keep records. It wasn't like this here; I sat for hours, against my back the heat of the refrigerator.

You dedicated this novel to "A"? the interviewer asked. Can you talk about that?

Yes, but I didn't write it for her, I said. It was just afterward, that I dedicated it, because I knew I should have.

Should have...?

She was so slow. Should have written it for A, I said.

I am no different from anyone, I said, after a pause. I was thinking of that journalist: I threw up outside after, he'd said, standing before the slideshow, on the screen one body's imperfectly closed eyes, lids too swollen. He thought we would sympathize. But you were one of the last people to see them, I thought. Didn't you owe them more, than to let disgust be your last gesture, the last thing they were offered? To sit and watch them, watch the flesh bruise and dampen on the stone, what had been blossoming becoming decay, no one coming through that place to tidy, and why should they tidy?—that's not what we owe each other.

S

At the shelter one kid had a horrendous infection that had started with a piercing. The other nurses were annoyed by him—He won't take it out, one complained as she led me to him, it's hopeless.

It's hardly hopeless, I said, I mean, I don't think he's going to die on us.

You know what I mean, she said. You deal with him.

The piercing was a bar through the top of the ear, a ball bearing outside each curve, inner and outer. Around the bar the ear was discolored and so saturated with pus it seemed in danger of becoming pure infection, something less than skin.

We'll have to take that out, I said, or you'll lose the ear.

I don't want to, he said.

So I hear, I said, but now there's no choice. I was putting on gloves. Unfortunately, it will hurt, I said, twisting a ball bearing with a set of small pliers we'd found just for this. The pus made them keep slipping.

It already hurts, he said.

It's a fucking mess, I said, looking at the tips of the fingers of the gloves.

I thought this was one of those Christian places, he said.

It is.

But you swear.

I do, I said, and got a firm grip on one ball bearing; he flinched.

Fuck, he said.

See how it is, I said. You know, you can get the other one pierced once you're better—and the ear was bleeding now, the blood slick with pus.

I liked it on the left, he said, and his eyes had tears in them I pretended not to see. The left and right aren't the same, he said.

That's absolutely true, I said. I could pull the bar free now, the blood more and more, the ear such a strange little piece of flesh, I was thinking, as it folded under my fingers, maybe the cartilage itself had lost integrity. I'm sorry, I said.

He didn't answer.

Did you like it? he said, and I wasn't sure, given how much he was crying, how he even knew to use the past tense. I was done, it was true: once I got the ball bearing to unstick from my gloves I dropped it in to clink in the metal dish on the tray.

Sure, I said.

The cotton balls shrank into red instantly.

I have to say, I'm not much for piercings, I said, I like to leave well enough alone.

I wanted to hold him gently by the chin but instead handed him a tissue.

•

Viv had always hated that phrase, *well enough alone.* That's no kind of vision, she said, who wants as little as *well enough*?

Who gets what they want? I asked her.

She shook her head. One shouldn't moderate desire by expectation. No hope in that. Nothing is well enough; leave nothing alone.

And this was a manifesto, but this was before Z died. Later I would say to her: We don't need more words for anything. As I walked down that hallway to see Z's body, footsteps echoing as in a bad movie.

I had pictured Viv's head nestled near my collarbone. This isn't what happened. Instead I put a hand just where Z's hand was so often, on her elbow.

·

She comes through town now sometimes, and sometimes I see her. If I saw her more often, what would be different? When she was sick I listened and I didn't quiet her. Her tongue grew dry. Her words were words like I'd never known, nothing staunched them. Talk yourself hoarse, I thought, as she began again. Her words left no residue. The eyes red after weeping, the salt that stays in the vision, the salt on the cheeks a tongue could note.

Z listened, I know.

Leave well enough alone, I think, my hand on a wrist's pulse, the corner of a book. We are instructed: fingers leave oil that eats away at monuments; fingers have diseases on them impossible to see.

# V

Ford said: A museum.

You don't mean that, A said.

I agree, I said. A museum.

I had been to Berlin and seen the Babylonian gate: it was housed in its own wing on an island mid-river in a foreign city. When, following your museum map, you turn the corner to see it, it's bigger and bluer than you could have thought. The tiles stretching endlessly, cobalt and smooth.

I described it to them. There was an enormous corridor leading down to the gate through the desert, it cannot be imagined. Of course they can't reconstruct the whole thing; there's a portion preserved, and then a model. And along the walls, in relief, lions, aurochs, mythical creatures. The people would stand in rows, the animals to their backs, in the heat, the blue shining, watching the king's procession.

Even the replicas have been looted, Ford said. The ones left on the original sites.

Is the aurochs a mythical creature? A asked.

No, I said, it's real.

Are you proposing we all fly to Europe and destroy a museum wing? Sara said.

You have a very literal mind, I told her.

·

Outside the museum, children had scattered from their school groups, backpacks in bright colors, shrieking and goading pigeons into flight. In many languages teachers tried to bring them to order. I sat on a café patio taking notes, the other tourists smoking and drinking sparkling water, the tabletops all sticky.

Were the other creatures dragons, Z asked, the ones in relief?

I had forgotten he had been there with me, that whole trip.

No, I said, that's not right, too European.

Though when I thought about it, that's how I remembered them too.

·

Where had I read: children gathered in the sewage-filled streets to throw stones at a tank. Which would swivel its gun toward them, but never fire. One day a stone might shoot right down the gun barrel, obstruct it. This isn't impossible—so many other things happened, almost everything, if you think about it.

# A

A school.

I don't remember who suggested it. We'd been up too long, crickets crowding at the windows, no one had moved in hours.

What? Sara said.

A student was beheaded last week, V said. A group of armed men went into the school and beheaded him.

For what? Sara said.

For nothing, I said. What could it be for?

His brother was in a militia, F said. The brother was who they wanted. The brother's militia came by later and hanged the guys who'd done the beheading outside the school, eight of them.

Jesus, I said.

I focused: But what could be the point of a school *here*?

That nothing's safe? Sara said. But that's crazy—

That we fail to learn, Z said.

Terrorism makes bad poetry, V said, leaning down to feed a scrap to the dog.

This isn't a joke, Z started—

I'm very serious, V said. It's interesting to consider whether this is more the terrorists' fault or the poets'. I blame the poets. As for bombing a school, I agree with Sara: it's insane.

No one would be hurt, F said.

What's hurt? Who's no one? V said.

It's not right to make everything into some game you play with words, F said.

How about a game you play with people? V said.

S

A bookstore! I said, and waited. We were all at A's, assembled.

It's already a cliché, Vivienne said—pages burning, which means history; covers burning, which are skin.

But that's all kind of true, A said.

Was this Sara's idea? Ford said.

Yes, I said.

He raised his eyebrows.

Yes, we could burn books, Viv said. History has established that—where they burn books they will soon burn people? Isn't that it? So we burn books to observe that in fact we've already burned people, whole cities, but no one paid attention. That this is how backwards it's all become.

Interesting, Ford said.

That it's hard to tell effects from causes, A said. Do clichés become true or do true things become clichés?

That it's hard to tell books from people, Viv said.

Or extremely easy, Z said, looking at her.

But you recognize, Viv went on, that the confusion is real. When you set fire to one book, you can't say it wasn't another. Just as years from now, you won't remember who started this conversation.

I will, I said.

Probably you won't, A said.

I already thought about all this, Ford said.

Really?

A bookstore, yes.

Did you? V turned toward him. Will my books be in it? I'll be furious. I'm already furious.

Well, not really, she added.

Everyone says there are too many books in the world, I said.

People also say there are too many people, Z said, but we draw a line.

We do, but not everyone does. These are real differences, A said, sounding too satisfied.

# A

In college Sara and I lived on the same hall. We weren't friends yet: she had a stiffness to her. Anyone could recognize her from behind as she walked, so upright, down the hall in her white bathrobe, hair swept up in a towel, shower caddy in hand. We smiled hello; if we were next to each other at the sinks in the morning brushing our teeth, we nodded.

She just happened to be there that afternoon. I'd been having this pain in my abdomen, a sharp pain wrapped in wet tissue, that's how it felt. It had ached for days. I'd called and made an appointment. But then I was standing in the shower and hit the wall hard with my hand. I had to look down to know there was blood, along my leg into the drain, it had felt no different from water. But the pain was sharp, then sharper. I turned the water off and hesitated.

Are you all right? Sara said. She was right outside the curtain.

I hesitated. I—

But she'd already flicked the curtain open. She was calm, her flat calm cheekbones. I have always looked at them first, this is why so often we failed to look right at each other.

I could see the blood, she said.

I don't think it's—

It's too fast anyway, she said, We have to go to the emergency room.

Once she took over, it was simple. She handed me my towel, left and came back with some clothes and a friend's car keys.

We sat in the ER waiting room together. She had gone to the triage window and explained.

I filled two pads with blood in the car on the way over. Just change them in the backseat, she said, There's a plastic bag.

I came home with my pills and instructions and the next night she knocked on my door, textbook in hand. I understood more quickly than she explained it to me, but is that so bad? Would you like some tea? I asked her. Chamomile, she said, which I'd been given a box of but hated. So it was her tea now, she started coming by almost every night to drink it.

She told me the most gruesome things, what she was learning every day. Sometimes I'd be high and hungry but she'd come by to talk about fistulas, about all the things that can go wrong with any baby, about what trickles out all the time. It's an easy surgery to fix it, she said, But thousands of women don't get it, they don't have access.

Easy surgery was never a phrase that made sense to me. I looked at my hands.

Access, I said out loud slowly, thinking of our drive to the hospital, how hard I had been trying to keep from bleeding on the seats.

You're so stoned, she said, just realizing.

I'm sorry, I said.

We were friends then.

# F

Jay and I used to bike to the gravel pits, past the *No Trespassing* signs. He biked right past and I followed. But when trucks came he was the one pulling me belly down into the gravel. You can't let them see you, he said. What do they care, I said. We were just kids. But when we biked down the pit's sides the gravel skidded out under our wheels, you could see we had been there: heaped-up spots and spots we'd splayed out in.

His hand on my back, stomach pressed against the gravel, head down. I remember this fear, it still comes back to me. I get it most when I'm filling out forms—it doesn't make sense, but it's what Jay left me with. I filled out so many forms for him. Trying to get him checked in, trying to get him whatever. He wouldn't do it. He wouldn't answer me either, he'd try to leave, that's when I'd have to hold him, when I had to start calling our friends to fight him back into whatever building.

We need that form, the receptionist said, I'm sorry.

We need a fucking tranquilizer, I said.

Jay was already in the parking lot, I could hear the shouting and car doors.

I'm sorry, I said to the receptionist. She hadn't been rude.

We just need to know what he's on, she said.

He's definitely drunk, I said. Maybe he's on some antidepressants.

He really shouldn't drink if—she started.

Jesus Christ, I said.

Sorry, I said to her or whoever in the lobby, put the clipboard down and went outside. Jay was leaning on the car, my dad standing next to him, not touching him.

I put my hand on Jay's shoulder and he shoved me off.

·

Now I fill everything out too fast, I don't even read, I hand whatever clipboard back over.

You didn't finish, they say to me, pointing at the blank lines.

But I won't, I am making my point.

S

It was my fourth time in a year giving blood and I wanted to shake a finger at people I passed on the street, people who passed the sign shouting BLOOD NEEDED in red letters. I don't even like doing it, and the headache afterward lasts days. But people are dying, I should have announced. The blood drive was too timid about it. I'd read that in Fallujah men had lined up to donate, not wanting to wait and so sticking the needles in themselves and pumping their fists. The Americans had just begun the siege of the city.

After I've donated I take a pastry and sit in the lobby. I should hurry back to work but today I don't care, I don't see why everyone there isn't here with me. I have to remind them: I leave notes on the refrigerator and bring it up too often. While around me in the lobby are a middle-aged woman in a pantsuit with shoulder pads, an old man, too old, I'd have thought. Two teenage girls looking pale, arms linked, drinking Hi-C. Why? I want to ask them all. Who have you lost?

Maybe no one, maybe it's just an idea of something good. On TV they see doctors hanging the bags, shouting, gurneys barreling, all that.

Those men, pumping their fists.

Most of that blood would have been wasted. During the siege there was almost no electricity, doctors worked by flashlight and cigarette lighter. They ran hot water over bags of blood to thaw them. The blood had been in the fridge where they used to keep lunches. How long does it take blood to spoil?—I don't know this; I should.

The teenage girls poked at each other's Band-Aids. Shiny silver. I'd been given a plain one.

I didn't want to go back to work, to lunchtime, the other women sitting around that table. This whole week the TV in the corner of the break room had been playing the same clip again and again: a new terrorist statement, according to the news. The terrorist's face appeared in the background, his beard, his calm hollowed eyes, his musical language, tripping up the throat lightly like a stream over stones, like the sound of a gun cocking. I've never heard a gun do this, only on TV. The translation scrolled across the bottom of the screen.

I can't believe they haven't caught him, someone said, All these years, and there he is, looking so smug.

He didn't look smug to me. His words sounded like the caves where they used to say he was. Round syllables one could slip into, then that harsh close in the throat, a dark wall in the back. I liked to hear it. I had always meant to learn it.

If I'd learned it I could have gone to that country.

I wanted to correct the women in the lunchroom, I wanted to leave notes on the refrigerator or folded into their lunch bags. The number of ambulances turned back from a checkpoint that day. How long between when a hospital ran out of antibiotics and more arrived. How do you clear the throat of vomit without electricity?

My phone was buzzing. Work, wondering would I be back soon. A patient was asking for me, they said. I got up, started the walk back in the sun. My head throbbed.

You gave blood? one of the volunteers asked when I got back to the shelter. Aren't you good, she said.

I shrugged.

# V

If, for instance, I were to go to a party. This is something that really happens; I am invited to them. I wear the right dresses, and later I dab traces of the evening out—red wine; a sauce that slipped through the fingers and smelled of fish; other people's perfumes, freesia, bay rum.

I might be invited to read. My voice always shakes, I can't help it, I keep water or wine close at hand, but my voice quivers. The air quivers with it, it descends, I look at the audience. Their faces and the shadows beneath their gestures, the flesh beneath the jaw just loose enough to allow speech—this is how it seems.

At a party, for instance, I might cross the room to admire a grandfather clock in the corner. The hour has passed but the clock doesn't chime; no one sits on the couches. We skim hands over each other: the back in first greeting, the forearm when, after several interruptions, we discover one another in conversation again.

My agent is here, a handful of publishers, writers I've met many times: friends. I take a glass from a tray. When I look at my agent, I think: we used to talk on the phone every day. This was just after Z died. She squeezes my hand warmly in passing. She won't stop for me, she's going to make small talk here and there, but she does this on my behalf, *Your mission: to tolerate*, she whispers as she passes, her earrings swinging forward. It's possible I'm too drunk.

It was a beautiful reading, someone says to me.

I have a beautiful mind, I want to say.

I have no patience for any of it. I ought to find the kitchen, be useful. Wipe lipstick off glasses and eat the broken spinach pies, something.

It wasn't that Z was good at these events; one couldn't say that. He was stiff; he was blunt; he disagreed. People learned to be wary of him, how he would turn his full power on any small remark, anything anyone would say idly. Their politics were nothing next to his, just what one would expect, thin and soggy. He could talk to anyone, though, his head tipped slightly to the side. I spent hours keeping an eye on him wondering when he might be offending. I think I loved it, people's variations of discomfort, but their feeling—palpable from across a room, palpable because I knew it—that they weren't free to leave, that it wouldn't be right not to listen, to endure.

·

Of course this isn't true exactly; there would only have been one or two such events in that time, when he was with me; neither of us was well known then, we weren't invited to many things. We went to a handful of places, but clung to each other in the corners, mouselike in the brightness. To shake hands Z had to slip his hand free of my elbow.

We would have been something else now. People would recognize my name when introduced. People would know his work. He would argue less; he could be beatific.

No one asks me outright about him; I don't know who even knows of him, sometimes an old acquaintance might venture something. Perhaps after a few more years they'll be bolder.

But—how people watch me. Tipsy in conversation I turn my head too quickly then must pause. Blood rises and pulses in the ears, in the delicate pouching under the eye it twitches. She is older, they think, she is getting on. Perhaps they explain to the new arrivals: She is the one whose lover—would they use this word?—and they'd point. This must be one reason people know me, though they don't admit it. Isn't she...? someone might ask. Or perhaps they don't talk about me at all, perhaps they invite me only out of obligation and hope that I'll say one clever thing lightly.

But they shouldn't expect this of me; Z was the light. Laughing I was still the shadow to him, how branches when backlit are cut so clear. This is the truth of me standing anywhere with anyone, shifting my weight and smiling, waiting to throw into the flame a twist of phrase, dry and snapping, how dutiful I've always been, doing my part to combat silence.

# A

At Jay's funeral I was Ford's girlfriend, that was my part.

F didn't talk to me, but we stood next to each other. The grandparents kept looking at my bare legs. I'd thought it was too hot for stockings, but their eyes were worse. I could feel the sweat on my back, drops along my legs one by one. The heels of my pumps stuck in the yard. I gathered armfuls of plates, trying not to tip the sandwich ends and white juice of potato salad back toward me. I filled garbage bags.

Once F reached over and pulled my dress off the small of my back to unstick it.

Sara arrived and hugged us each a long time. She walked over the yard to shake the hands of the relatives. She had worn sensible shoes.

Five or six men from Jay's unit had come. They stood close together and cried more than I'd expected. What did I know? But I'd never pictured them crying. The sun was hot and the back of one man's neck was burning. Another man rubbed up and down one arm with his hand, a strange nervous gesture. A civilian gesture, I thought, he couldn't have done it when in gear. I took them a tray of lemonade.

They thanked me in turn.

How are those shoes working for you? one said, eyeing my heels as I wobbled.

I shook my head and smiled, then wondered if that was the wrong response. I started walking away, then turned back.

Would you like chairs? I offered.

F was sitting on the tree stump. There were some folding chairs out, but the older relatives were sitting in them.

We're fine, one guy said.

There's more, I said, We could bring them out for every-body.

So two of them followed me into the house, down the stairs into the basement. We took the chairs out, me two at a time, them four. The metal slicked up in my palm and slid; I had to keep hitching the chairs up with each hip. You got those? one of the men said, putting his chairs down, reaching around me to open the door.

Yes, thanks, I said. But I didn't, they were slipping again.

Here, he said, and took a handkerchief out of his pocket, offered it to me.

I looked at it for a second.

To wipe your hands with, he said, and the chairs, get the sweat off.

Right, I said, and smiled again, then wondered again if I should have. I rubbed the handkerchief across my palm, be-tween the fingers. Maybe it helped.

He was watching me, a little smile.

How did you know Jay? he said.

I went to school with his brother, I said.

The smart one? he said. That's what Jay always said, his brother was supersmart.

He can be, I said.

We were standing in the doorway, he was still holding open the door.

Were you in touch? I asked, I mean, you and Jay—

He shook his head.

I didn't know him that well, I said, I don't think I ever even saw him sober.

Funny, I don't think I ever saw him drunk, he said. He patted me on the shoulder as if I were younger than I was.

# F

There are things I can admit now—I call and try to say them to A. I know, I already knew that, she says, because now she can be like this. I say: You know how it is in those countries where there's no news, not really, all the papers are state-owned and every day they say the same thing?

I just wanted to tell you.

A doesn't understand.

We took that country easily. From the way they talked about it it seemed almost as easy there as it was for us here. A few weeks and it was over. Foreign troops marched right up the streets. Just a day or two before, the information minister had been on TV saying: *We will slaughter them and bury their bodies in our soil.* But he knew his country was defeated.

I saw A's notebooks if she left them open, if the dog knocked them off the table, but she only wrote about things like: an old election sign she'd seen in an alley, a worm curled across its surface after the rain. How the light framed each finger on V's hand as V moved a wet branch aside. Things like this. Which were true but weren't—

Put it this way: I hated.

I hated the rallies on TV. Waves of red, white, and blue balloons undulating. I hated the faces of the men speaking, president, vice president, all the rest. I agreed with the strident middle-aged women who gathered outside shrieking, holding signs. Shouting, not ululating. They had websites. They were a movement. I didn't join them but—I thought of those waves of balloons breaking.

It had in fact happened: someone handed a flower to a soldier.

The soldiers tossed packaged meals to the people, but the people hadn't been starving.

I watched those men talk and talk about this new country. Whose name they wouldn't say right, pronounced it with a twang like a wink.

The newspapers debated the politicians' stances, reported on their disagreements. The newspapers reported where the politicians would be the next day and they were. We lived somewhere this safe: even years later, long defeated, these men's faces wouldn't be photographed light-dazzled and bearded after months underground. Then hooded. When their time was up they turned and waved and got on a plane. They got older. There would be stories in the newspapers about them decades later, if they opened a library, wrote a book, or died.

I only wanted—I said, and waited for her to say something.

·

A construction site, Z said one night. By then it was just the two of us, in the basement of the new house.

I knew why he'd thought of it; for once I wasn't impressed. The night before we'd driven by a construction site on our way back from an antiwar meeting. A waste of time, Z said, fuming in the passenger seat. I'd slowed down as lanes merged, and then on our left there were gold sparks, bright in the dark, arching over the torso of a workman bending down. I thought we could even hear the sparks snap, but afterward I could only remember the thump of the drilling, Z's voice, and the bugs in the ditches keening.

The burst of light surprised us both, we both turned. Watch the wheel, Z said, and grabbed it with one hand.

The guardrail glowed yellow, then we'd passed.

Why? I asked him the next night.

Those sites are the maintenance of the status quo, he said. They're thoughtless, totally mechanical: without thinking about what's needed, what could be done differently, is there another way, they just pay to get the job done, keep things going. Do you see?

It should be one by the side of the road, he added, so people can see it as they drive by, what's left of it. Wonder why.

I can't see how that would even work, I said, I mean, that's kind of what construction sites always look like.

We argued, we moved on.

I told him: I'd worked construction in the summers as a teenager, building concrete roads. One day I'd been out with a jackhammer breaking up the old road, then put my foot too far forward. The bit hit the boot's steel toe, and there were sparks, a gold cloud of them shooting up my leg toward my face. I watched them a second, felt the heat, before I moved. Shit, you all right? someone called to me, and I stepped back and was.

# V

The interviewer and I have been sitting for what feels like hours, the room getting warm.

She asks: Who are your greatest influences?

I give her some names, but say—of course it's easy to be influenced by the dead. You don't have to wonder what they think. When they come and visit you, in bed, again, stuck there, what do they say to each other after they've left? As they sit together all those nights without you. Z chopping the basil he coaxed up from a few window boxes, cooking something he may bring you later, but you won't eat.

I don't really say this.

Do you have any advice for young writers? she asks.

If you have to raid a hospital, don't tie the hands of the doctors trying to cut an umbilical cord. Just let them finish.

But if you had to give—

I never mean to be difficult. It's just that I falter. I make a mug of tea and forget where I've left it. I say I want to have Z's body cremated, and don't think how there wouldn't be a grave to go to.

I've forgotten the sound of Z's skin against mine.

What is your next book about?

As a child I found my mother crying in front of the mirror at her vanity table.

When you were sick she sat for hours by your bedside.

Yes, and still I have not dedicated anything to her.

You say you wouldn't have minded about the blood.

No, just the child's crying. And then the mother.

The mother?

I don't know what happened to her.

# A

V and I sat in her living room. Do you ever think of travel-
ing? I asked V.

And who would take care of me, if I got sick in some other
country?

But you hardly get sick anymore, you live by yourself here,
I said.

But I know I always could—she smiled and ran her fingers
over my knuckles, my hand was on the couch between us.

It seems good for writing, I said, and Z—

The other month when I was sick, she said, I lay in the
garden by the clothesline. I'd washed the blankets a few days
before, but then I was sick, I didn't feel like dealing with anything, I couldn't. So I left the blankets out and it rained every
night. They were mildewing. Later I lay in the yard looking at
the corner of one blanket where a spider had laid a sac of eggs.
The spider was this translucent green-yellow, the sort of color
that looks completely eerie in daylight. The egg sac was like this

too, but whiter. Around it the smallest web was stretched over the fabric. The spider didn't move at all, just sat by the egg sac. The blanket smelled, I could smell it from where I was.

I waited.

What I mean is, she said, I didn't travel to see it and I can say so little about it.

I understand that, but—

I know, she said, I'm impossible, irritating.

But really, she said, what do you even think of palm trees?

They always look fake to me, I said.

Snow-topped mountains?

I've seen those, but I was a child. I think of them as something I could have made up.

I've seen them too, she said, but yes, the same.


She said: Those rocks—erratics?—right on the very brinks of cliffs, they say glaciers left there?

Implausible, I said, a cartoon of an ice age.

That they can pull the brain out through the nose to mummify someone?

I didn't use to believe that, I said, but now I can see it. But did anyone ever believe the dead spent the coin left on the tongue?

It's a nice gesture, V said.


That they boil silkworms alive to make blankets, I said.

Fine, V said, of course they do.


Children talking in other languages, she said.

Gibberish, I said.

I said: The bombs they meant for the dictator's sons didn't kill them, but killed another family—a man who lived in the same neighborhood as a restaurant where the dictator's family liked to go—the bomb killed his seven nieces and nephews. He found their bodies in the crater.

V said: That would take me a while to believe, a day or two, or much longer.

But, she said after a while, I believe they killed the dictator's sons another way eventually.

Of course they did, I said.

# V

My morning walk takes me through the cemetery, a joke with myself. Doctors tell me to walk every day: here I am. To my health.

Around the graveyard there's a split-log fence, ineffectual, traditional; the whole place a floodplain. Northward levees hold the river in tight curves, houses crowd the levees, backyards and swing sets, children kick into the sky above the river.

And every morning I walk toward the graveyard, let myself in by the gate; no matter how I tire of it, every day.

The earth sinks beneath me. Under my weight I believe the hollows made for the dead give. The ground can't reclaim its firmness; the roots of cypresses strain to unearth the fence.

One pictures the flesh as it is in movies, straggling on a slim femur, the elegance of the hip bone, pelvis. I walk above this and so press down into; I add my weight to these processes, I don't know them; nitrogen, roots, water to sky and down again over or through.

There are stones I used to read that are now illegible.

I think of bodies in ditches. What distinguishes ditch from grave is mere deliberation; that soothing of earth, ordering. This is a place for death, here; that, a place for runoff, trash, plants that flourish in the blend of mud and exhaust, song of crickets, toads. Salamanders cross the road slowly, one must spot them in the headlights and stop. The ditches are where bombs are planted, where ambushes wait, where bodies roll to naturally: the lowest point. I can understand this the way these things are explained, how over time stars move farther from each other but somehow not closer to anything else, how molecules hit and hit and then slow, having exchanged what they had enough motion for. I do not understand this; I do not know how different the tongue may be, for instance, than the skin on the back of the hand, which may last longer underground. I don't know how to build a bomb that would detonate with the pressure of a passing car.

There are things we can learn.

What is the opposite of entropy? What allows things to fall back to us, reprise?

Beneath us water is still but holds something of rainstorms—

Beneath us the tongues endure or don't—

Graveyards, crickets, wind in trees—all could be called quiet; no one hears what has been rigged under the roads.

# A

A cemetery, V said, from her chair in the corner.

The dog stirred and Sara scratched his neck.

Tell me more, F said, lifting a plate away from V; she had been dragging a fork over it ceaselessly.

You're not going to tell me how disgusting an idea it is? Hateful? V said, turning toward him, her neck stretched over the armrest.

No, go ahead, F said. Tell me how we should blame the dead.

Not the dead themselves—V sat up—but how we honor them. How we're told they died for our freedom. It's as bad as dying for our sins.

No, F said, sin is—

If it's real freedom then we should be free from them. If we're not free to choose, free to violate, then they died for nothing.

I said: But really they just died in the wars they were sent to.

They both looked at me, annoyed.

The families would hate you, F said to V.

It's not as though I'd sign my name to it, she said, It's a bombing, not something you publish.

Gravestones broken up, she said, toppled in, the bones all mixed.

For what it's worth, F said, I might hate you.

But that doesn't matter, V said.

# A

You think that if something happens only once, there's a way in which it didn't happen. I was at the kitchen window, watching a man in a red tracksuit walk down the street. He was walking slowly, jacket rustling over his belly. He may have been going to the trails, dressed brightly for hunting season.

Z was over, waiting for F, wanting to talk about something. He got a glass of water and stood next to me by the window. What is it? he said. I had been holding my mug and staring, not drinking.

I was reading, I said, They say they buried people in a stadium by description, there was no time to identify them. *An old man in a blue tracksuit*, that was one of the graves.

His tracksuit's red, Z said, nodding at the man outside.

We were in front of the window where anyone could see, but no one was there. The man had passed. When Z turned toward me I kissed him. Z's smooth cheeks, his hair that smelled of the candles Vivienne burned.

# F

I could revise, I think I said to A on the phone.

You're high, she said.

No, I said, without thinking about whether it was true.

It doesn't matter, I said, I think about it all the time.

About what? she said. Stop, she said to the dog on the other end of the phone, meaning whatever he was peeing on. I only ever called A right before I went to bed, which was morning her time. I liked to hear her walking the dog, feet shuffling in the leaves.

Leave it, A said to the dog.

What was it? I asked.

Chicken bone, she said—What is it you're always thinking about?

It's all just revision, I said.

She was silent.

I mean, even if you change everything, it's like revising.

Sure, she said.

Since when are you a writer? she said when I paused too long.

I applied at a newspaper, I said.

What?

The interview was rough. It's just an alternative weekly, entry-level position. Maybe I'd cover some science, but I mean, they were right about me not having experience. I had some things to say, though.

What did you say?

Mostly what Z said. About how objectivity is the worst lie of all.

But you're not going to be some foreign correspondent.

No, I said, and I was scooping coffee into the filter paper, it might not be a night for sleeping—But I could cover this city. I'd like that.

You could get people to talk to you, she said.

I think I have this voice like his voice in me, I said, I mean Z.

I have, she said, and paused. There was a siren in my distance or hers.

What? I said.

I have a voice like your voice in me, she said. Always telling me to write.

Did I tell you to write?

You did.


Didn't we talk about a newspaper office once? I asked—A had a mind for history.

Yes, she said.

The paper burning, I said.

Yes, she said.

But there's no point, really, I said. It's the TV stations more. Yes, more harm than good.

If you can even do those kinds of equations, I said, calculate degrees of harm.

I think so, she said.

No, I said. You can't, it doesn't work that way. These kinds of things, actions, insurrections, you just do them or you don't. That's it.

Just yes or no, black or white, day or night? she said.

I was yawning.

I—I started, but she was talking to the dog again. Good night, I said, and she laughed.

# A

A real estate office, F said.

You already said that, V said.

What are you talking about? Z said. His fingers drummed across my coffee table.

I was just talking—F started.

How surprising, V said.

F wasn't angry. I always forgot how hard it was to make him angry.

Before I was just talking, he said, but right now I was thinking about how we all move, just pick up and move all the time.

Yes? Z said.

I mean, we're not driven out, we just go to go.

I guess you could put it that way, Z said.

Why should we have that privilege? F said. I could have stayed in the same town my brother and I grew up in, but I didn't. I just left.

Not *just*, Sara said.

It was easy, F said.

And it shouldn't have been? Sara asked.

My point is, the privilege, F said. Our freedom, running around like—

Don't think you have all the freedom you think, Sara said.

Yes, Z said.

What do you mean? F asked.

What I said, Sara said. I have to go.

To work, she added, getting up. Nothing more exciting.

# V

Now the oregano is overgrown, soon the mint. I am tending to the garden Z planted but don't have Z's touch. He hung tinfoil to scare off the deer. He came inside, a pumpkin in his hands, from the corner where when I'd last thought to look there had been only pumpkin flowers.

He left sweet pea flowers in a vase by our bed.

·

A hospital, I said.

Their silence was what I wanted.

I wanted them to get up and leave me, I would lean my forehead against the window and listen to the rain, listen to the moths hitting the window through the clear nights when there was no other light, neighbors gone to bed hours earlier.

We'd read: In Baghdad the hospitals were too full and there were too few doctors.

It is a rule, hospitals are not targets.

To think of the landscape this way, divided into target, not target. I might look out the window. The squirrels move with a speed I think of as guilty. People shoot deer from their gardens.

What I mean is: the hospital is where plans go awry, where plans are wasted. One plants rows but weeds come in. Bitterness in the mouth, staring at the ceiling. The inked fingertips that were supposed to mean one thing, were declaimed by TVs and newspapers to mean one thing, had instead become a target.

A hospital. Z started to collect me that night. To put my words into something he could bury, something he could love better. Let's pretend Vivienne didn't say—the rows of the sick, the mothers in the throes of childbirth. Let's pretend, Vivienne. It's time to go, he said, or something like this, and Sara was stacking glasses inside one another to take to the kitchen.

But I meant it, I said.

No one answered.

My words are fireflies in jars, I thought. A light people like to look at but don't see by.

I meant: an end to all this waste. Men come into schools midday to set fire to the hair of the girls who don't wear headscarves. Let's not pretend we could ever say, this won't happen, or that. That doctors won't be about to cut an umbilical cord when soldiers tie their wrists. Those nights Z's hand lay upon my stomach.

I execute a plan and publish it.

Someone might execute this doctor, this farmer, an artist, to be found later with the shells of the bullets that killed him tucked in his pockets.

What I was saying: all rules have been broken. Every story proves only myth.

A poison in the shells of the eggs, a sky that broke into storm.

What I would have given, those hours staring at the ceiling. For an end. This may be true, yes, but this is not what I mean. What I mean is only the truth of these hours. The date palms plowed under, bodies that won't even nourish the cypresses. I want the dust of that place on my skin, in my pockets. This is all I meant.

# A

An end, I said.

What, like a funeral? Z said.

Vivienne frowned: A funeral isn't an end, it's to witness an end. To acknowledge the fact of ends. It's not the same.

The difference between communion and transubstantiation, Sara said.

Please, F said, Don't start.

I said: I read in the newspaper that they're withdrawing 3,500 trucks of materiel every night. Mortar shells, coffeemakers, everything.

Most of that is going to the other war, Z said.

I know. Not an end in sight.

There was a short silence. V laughed. And then I found twenty bucks, she said.

We looked at her.

It's a way to end, she said, that's all. When a story hasn't come off like you wanted.

S

There was a kid in the shelter with shingles. We had to keep him separated from everyone; I went to visit him as often as I could. There wasn't much to say, so we played Connect Four, which he was surprisingly bad at.

We sat across from each other, the plastic contraption on the table between us. His room had no windows and he never turned the TV off.

It was a soap opera, I saw when I looked over, and this was kind of endearing. I looked back at him. One hand was playing one of the plastic checkers across the table, the other was picking at his face.

I'm too old for chicken pox, he said, and dropped a checker into a slot. I could picture my victory—I dropped my checker and it clicked.

It's not the same, I said. Same virus, different disease.

Same thing, he said, looking at the finger that had been scratching his face: All these fucking spots.

I leaned toward him, toward the drop forming on his forehead, half pus, half blood, the translucence and redness distinct.

That, I said, is just a pimple you've been picking at. Which you're definitely not too old for.

Shit, he said, and laughed. Way to be nice about it. He leaned back to get a tissue, which he pressed to his forehead.

I shrugged.

You must think I suck at this game, he said, dropping a piece into the worst possible position.

I smiled and shrugged again.

I always used to lose to my sister on purpose, he said. So I guess that's how I like to play.

That's sweet, I said.

No, she hated it, that's why I did it. She used to bitch about it to our mom. But she couldn't do anything, no one can prove you're trying to lose. I'd just be like, no, I'm really that bad.

I'm not playing with you anymore, I said. He was already pushing the table back, hunching back up into his pillows to see the TV.

Yeah, I guess that's what I'm saying, it's not as fun with you, he said, grinning.

# F

In the middle of almost every night A woke up, thirsty, and I never understood it. Why don't you drink something before you go to bed? I asked her.

I'm not thirsty then, she said.

She said: Isn't it strange how you can't imagine drinking when you're thirsty, or heat when you're cold? You can't. You know what I'm talking about. When your wrists hurt so bad in the cold, and you think the water in you could freeze and your skin could just blow open?

Sure, I said.

But in the heat of a desert people don't know how that feels.

I guess not, I said.

You just can't imagine it, she said.

Another time as I heard her wake up, slip out of bed, I said, *Look to martyrdom as a thirsty man looks to water.* I thought she would ask me what I meant but she must not have heard.

She would leave her glass of water next to the bed just where I would tip it over if I got up in the night.

•

It's a saying there, I would have said, *Look to martyrdom*...

•

I wanted to pull on A's hip like a child—They're all refugees there, I said. Let's go. I don't mean go there—I said before she could argue. But let's go. To the tree houses you can find even in these woods. To the strip malls where farms were. The thing is, if we never saw Vivienne, Sara, Z, again, I wouldn't care. A would tell a story, Do you remember when Vivienne...? And I would but I wouldn't care.

In my dreams flames reached the ceiling of A's house. People die of smoke without waking.

•

A's hand on my shoulder, then gone again, A never remembering in the morning what we had said to each other at night. How did you sleep, she'd ask, as she came back in with the dog and I was putting on a new pot of coffee. Fine, I'd say, the dog as always trailing dead leaves in.

# S

I take long walks; it's pointless, but I am trying finally to love this city. I like—how down the middle of a block by my work I've discovered a hidden dirt road, covered with trash and weeds growing thickly, lush is the word. Two mattresses bloat side-by-side obstructing the way—as if it's a slumber party, I think, like a child. The top of one is torn open and smells of old rain. On the frame there's a slug at least six inches long, spotted across its back, tropical looking, trailing slime.

*Fuck the police*, someone has spray-painted on the fence. I could love this, too. It's harmless, that paint-can hissing sound. I heard it once as I rounded the shelter, my shift ending: kids were vandalizing the shelter's back brick wall. It was upsetting, would be expensive to deal with, but at the time, when I could only hear the laughter and the hiss, I smiled, I didn't think.

At the shelter everyone always feels more for the children. There are always shelters for children but men can be left on the street to ignore. I've never understood this. I argue with my parents when they say something about *the women and children*. The *civilian casualties*. All right, I say, there are three of us at the table. How is it different which two are left?

On the shelter wall the children had spray-painted: *JD sucks dick*. We had to hire someone to powerblast it off.

In the newspapers they said the woman who had been the most recent bomb had maneuvered by taking the hand of a child.

Today I see the shine behind a slug, that belled flower curling over a guardrail, a tricycle left in an alley, the child too big for it.

# A

I'm sure the four of us still read everything, follow all the news. I rely on this thought, I think of what I might say to them after I read anything: an article about the president's most recent speech. An interview with veterans. Debates on whether one should use the term *civil war*. An article on windmills, an article on centrifuges. On the screen the president gesturing, the assembly hall in Cairo packed full. The camera surveys: who cheers, who doesn't.

*But I also know that human progress cannot be denied,* he was saying.

You could call that love, Sara would have said.

•

In the newspapers a man walks out of the scene of the blast, a kerchief tied around his forehead and already bloodied, his face unrecognizable, if I had known him.

·

Love? I fear that I don't have it in me, to love in the right ways, the hardest ways. I would leave the doors open, let the children play wherever they wanted, on the side of whatever road. I wouldn't stop them, the teenagers, I'd let them go to any club, no matter the bombings in the news.

·

Did you know I've never been in love? Sara said once. What people would call *in love*.

What do they know? F said. Any of them.

·

If we had been there, after the blast, among the fragments of glass, looking around for each other.

# S

The other week I went to hear Vivienne read. I could have told her beforehand I was coming, but I didn't. I wanted to see her surprise, see the muscles of her face before she composes them, before she pushes her way half-elegantly through the small crowd to say hello. Is her expression sudden warmth or anxiety? I can't say. She sees me and it's as if we've discovered each other, each poised before a mirror.

Her voice shakes as she reads. It always has. She drinks at least three glasses of water. When she looks up at the audience, she looks right at me. I wonder who she looks at when I'm not there. Her eyes widen, her fingertips touch the pages. She doesn't falter, never interrupts herself, but her voice always thrums, I can see the pulse twitter in her throat.

Her sentences all sound like her—this isn't much of a response, but it's true and it's what I say to her. It sounds exactly like you, I say, and she smiles at me, that bird of a smile, tilting toward me then off again.

Thank you, she says, which she's been saying all night. She looks relieved. But a handful of people have already gathered beside her. She lays her hand on my arm, a gesture of affection that's not natural to her, too graceful. It would be more like her to tuck my hair behind my ear, to punctuate some comment with a little kick to Z's shin.

Do you mind if...? she says to me, and turns toward the people waiting. Or she might not say it, quite. I nod, I pick up her book and flip through, though I've already read it.

I invited the other women from work to come with me to the reading, knowing they'd say no.

Viv doesn't call me before she comes to town: either she knows I'll come or doesn't think of me.

I'm so glad you're here, she says to me afterward, and I know to believe her. We've stepped outside, are walking toward the bus stop. She'll go to some dinner—Do you want to join us? she asks me, and I believe she wants me to. She's walking very slowly. How are you feeling? I ask. She looks up quickly. Fine, she says—I'm almost never sick anymore. She slips her hand through my elbow. It's not that, she says, I was walking slowly because I figured you wouldn't agree to dinner, we would just have this walk.

She asks about my work, predictable questions. But she presses my arm hard, drums her thumb along it. We dawdle and then the walk ends.

It was a beautiful reading, I say.

I wish you would come, she says, pulling at my arm, then kissing my cheek and going.

# V

I've been asked to give a talk and I don't know the first thing. I should talk about the escalation in Afghanistan but I can't remember the right details. What is the name of the mountain range...? I can't call anyone to ask; I should just look it up; I do. I've sketched a little map on my desk but it doesn't seem to help.

Not a new war: growing.

A war doesn't grow, though, that's not the phrase: *escalate*. From: endlessly circulating stairs, a belt, mothers' eyes fixed on children's toes. From: *to climb a wall by ladder*. Backward, this evolution. Don't ladders and stairs occur naturally? One can find both in rock. Mountains especially. Man constructs his own version; then, to spare the effort, stairs that move themselves, so that one can ascend as easily as—fog lifting up a mountain slope, licking or gliding, however one would describe it. Thus a new verb is born.

Which then describes actions such as surges, or what, intensified bombing campaigns.

How did a war *grow*, then, before escalators? It didn't ascend; rather, perhaps, fields, widening. One thinks of Pennsylvania, the rolling hills. A war used to grow into earth, the dead buried, a root system. Or moved toward the sea: a war took route.

Now a war ascends, as though effortlessly.

No—through an artificial mechanism. Those toy AK-47s—or are they toy Kalashnikovs, properly?

Climbs toward what? A war digs in, a war sinks into. A war—not metastasizes, no; it's not right to quarantine it to a single body. A dandelion clock, blown, as though by a child. A trampling that disseminates.

Trampled down the vintage where the grapes of wrath, etc.

Is this what I ought to say, is this what I mean? Something like this. War has worked its way up, is no longer held to the earth. Journalists can be shot from Apaches. Bombs aimed through cloud cover. When it used to be: keeping the head low, feet damp and blackening in the trench, so that one couldn't distinguish ankle from earth from bacteria from anything, the only cure amputation. As though earth claimed those men piece by piece. Each soldier was granted one bayonet; he might cut off a hand and go home.

Now: a car *inches*—this is always the word, as though they progressed so endearingly: belly to earth, then arched, then humped forward—through traffic, stops. But the trunk is full of explosives. The building full of government workers, or children.

The blast walls have just been taken down.

Smoke visible on the horizon.

Against the horizon?

Against.

I realize: it's a valley I've forgotten the name of, that I keep meaning to write about, not the mountains. The fighters came down out of the mountains, claimed a valley, sent all the girls home from school.

And what do the girls do now? Sit at home and—cook? Is there food enough for these extra workers? Sewing?

War bores. War kneads. War stitches.

War doesn't escalate, but back-forms. A braid burned to scalp. A wall taken down, a car bomb takes down a building, maybe a government. I have drawn a map on my desk of places I won't live. I will talk about them. I will note that no one remembers when war was last in this country—nod to the windows, the past, the tents of brandied wounds, amputees, cholera, the hundreds of thousands dead, more of sickness than war itself. In those days, perhaps even I could have been among those tending. I could have gone as Sara would from tent to tent, hand on foreheads, blessing souls, believing perhaps as a member of that generation that souls when freed of their bodies ascend. Carrying of course the worst infections with me, in my aprons, clothes pus-stained, smell of gangrene in my hair, of course we can't imagine. In Pennsylvania a man came by train and made a speech that made history. I believe in the beauty of this: I am elevated. These fields sanctified, he said; no, he said, ourselves.

But if we die in another country? If war in taking root roots us to a soil we do not know? I am not there. I don't hear the wind dragging clouds over that valley, uprooting the canvas that had been staked, cooling the faces of those lying wide-eyed within.

S

I try to picture Z's face, but I can't. I see only the photo, the fine definition, his face turned away. A branch low over the sidewalk brushes my forehead coldly, I can smell the rain wounding the petals. I imagine Vivienne's hand lifting the branch for me to pass under.

The trees' spring vigor: roots drink the meltwater and sap rises.

Z is dead. And the rest of us, did we tire of each other? Or did we tire of everything else? We watched the news together, the shots of a street after any blast: mourning passed over the women's faces so quickly and into their open mouths. We can say that it is mourning, just as what occurs on that hillside is autumn.

I don't know.

I look forward to seeing anyone new at the shelter. I tried to talk about this once and the other nurses didn't understand—as though I were wishing homelessness on more people. No, not that. But I'd rather not see the same faces.

When someone new comes in, I tried to say, in that moment, we give comfort. Later we're merely routine—but think how nice that first night here, as I press the stomach softly with the butt of the hand, feel at the organs. Good, I nod.

We may or may not see each other again, any patient and I. They might go back home, to school, get a place with a friend, that kind of story.

I tried asking the other nurses: Don't you think it's strange that what we should most hope for is that one day we'll come in and no one will be here, in the whole city no one will need us?

No, one woman said, and she was probably right.

Of course I too want the routine, getting ready for work each morning. Of course it's worse to think of the fates of those who don't come in to the shelter. I've passed them, they sleep turned toward the metal of a bench. Sweatshirt pulled tight, so that it's impossible to know them by their features. Faces are a landscape it takes us so long to map, so that days pass before I can say which man I pass each morning. They don't remember me either. We duck under that tree branch in succession, in succession step over the root that erupts almost through the sidewalk. Our faces both touched by rain into deeper color. And I reach toward the damp flowers as Vivienne would.

# F

I try to write. Only when I know there isn't enough time, that I'll be interrupted. Yesterday on my lunch break. The other day as an egg cooked, I wrote a couple things on a piece of paper. Wrote idly—that's the word for it, leaning against the counter, still not sure how to start, the yolk heating into rubber. *He leans against the counter and writes a few things idly.*

Manifesto? This word was just a joke with A. Write a manifesto, I said, throwing my arms open some twilight, rabbits nibbling at the yard just to be near us, I think this is what she said, deer coming to worship. We'd had a *successful action*—Z's phrase. Back room of an abandoned political office, a right-wing politician who'd run the year before. The charge had been weak. It didn't look like I thought it would afterward. Ceiling held, walls erect. The room looked dirtied, the windows blown out. But the whole city was filled with boarded-up windows; from the outside you couldn't tell that building from anywhere. Except that the destruction was thorough, each window broken down to each corner and a black skin of dust over the room, the chairs thrown wide.

We sent a letter to the local paper explaining why we'd done it, but they didn't print it. It didn't occur to us they might not print it. We read the paper front to back for days. It was Z who said, Of course they didn't, so that we felt like children.

We were young. We fought over who would write the letter. I wanted A to. She did. Not like that, I said. Just be direct for once. You need to just say—

I did, she said.

No, you didn't. Start, *In protest of the brutal ongoing occupation*—you know what I mean.

We fought.

This is what I mean, she said. If you mean something else, you write it.

I did. Mine was short, to the point. I named the recent escalations. I gave statistics: articles, the pile of pamphlets I had from every clinic, every treatment center Jay had been to.

A read it over. She rewrote it for me, crushing her suggestions to fit between the lines. That sounds childish, she said, what about something like—

Childlike, I said. It is childlike. It's simple. Right and wrong. It doesn't have to sound intellectual. It's not.

They won't listen, though, she said, tapping her pencil. I knew she wanted to show Z, get him on her side.

I don't think you know who *they* are, I said.

What do you mean? she asked me. Or maybe it was: What?

Who we're talking to, I said. You're writing for yourself, I told her, but I am trying actually to communicate.

She went over her suggestions with me again. She thought I made her changes but I didn't. I sent the paper my version. I waited for the fight with her that would come when they printed it. But they never printed it.

I wanted her to try. To just say—

I wanted something, I tried to explain, small enough to fit in the hand. What does that mean? Something you could toss into the crowd, like the MREs soldiers threw, like a curse. A proverb, something to learn by heart. What anyone could remember and think to himself while walking down any street, something that would sum up the whole thing, the young men on this or that corner watching, rippling back into the buildings as Humvees passed, the men coming by houses rapping hard on a door they'd break down anyway. Something as firm and distinct as that rapping, a door knob, a gun butt, not a bullet, but a phrase like *Me and my brother against my cousin. Me and my cousin against a stranger.*

A prayer, A said.

Whatever, I said, fine, if it's the kind of prayer that's a demand. *God make us safe.*

That's not a demand, she said, it's not in the vocative.

Jesus Christ, I said.

My words all mean something, she said, that's why you ask me for them.

No, I said to her another time, rereading what she'd written, trying to convince her again. My hand on her shoulder as she sat at her desk. She put her hand on mine, but only to lift mine away.

Go back to your chem set, she said, leave me alone—not a prayer.

*Dear A*, I write, and write.

# A

I go weeks without reading the news so that when F calls I won't know what he's talking about. He'll get to explain it to me and I won't have to argue with him.

He doesn't call.

I don't read the news because it doesn't offer itself to me. I walk past the 7-11, a boy plays a harmonica, his stomach bunched up on his knees, his feet on the bench of a picnic table. I burned my notebooks because I didn't want them. No, because I was afraid.

F ran his hand along my arm, kissed the back of my neck, but he never *said*. I was always the one to say. Breath after breath and my blood shone with his motion. I didn't know my voice, I saw the ceiling above me, knew it as the pressure of his fingertips, the ceiling fan still and the curtain skimming the floorboards.

If my throat stained red, if my cheek did.

You are so quiet, I said to him.

So write about it, he might as well have said.

I will write a few things, I said.

.

Write it, A, you said to me, fingers black with newsprint. I pointed my toe at your hip, palm, temple, until I felt my bones soften again, your mouth full of my hair.

What is the point? I shook your face in exasperation. I could pile the words up by the side of the bed. But you would turn over to sleep. Never having explained anything—but you always told me, you would say. I love you, you said, and meant it. You mapped me but rolled up what you drew, tucked it where I wouldn't see it. Let's live here, you said, tracing an X along the stretch of belly, guarded by the quiet lookout of the hips. As though we had a choice.

They have to understand, you said, and I thought you meant the war, but you meant me. We found some buildings we could agree on. Or not. I thought I didn't know enough about that country—*let's go there*, but this was as your lips were pausing on my wrist. You meant where we were together. I must have always misunderstood. I am not alone in this, although I may be alone. Bodies that have spent years in apprenticeship to one another, then noted not that the fit was wrong but that what they'd meant to mold to, each uncompromised plane, they should have broken. I mean, what you wanted me to tell you. Was what you wanted me to write.

# V

I haven't been sick in years, I tell them, but still: a checkup.

They slide me into the MRI; they slide the cushion under the knees, the cushions next to the ears. From the corner a voice: *There will be a clicking sound. Try to keep still.*

The clicking is really a thumping, screeching and thunderous, but I don't mind. I lie there, still, sometimes I sleep.

Not many people can sleep through that racket, the technician says afterward, smiling, folding the blanket.

A beautiful brain, they have always told me, clicking through the images: soft gray clouds of flesh, thin white rim of skull. Lobes curve symmetrically toward the ears, down into the neck, the perspective shifts, click. I don't know how anyone can distinguish anomaly in this complicated perfection.

But this time they pause. There's one bright spot: they point at it on the films until it rainbows a little with the oils of their fingertips. What do you think of…? they ask each other. I watch.

On the film one can't see the eyes, just a graceful indentation, the space left for eyes within a skull.

The doctors discuss; I am silent. The brain is silent; the machine hums.

Beautiful, they have always nodded at my films before. Yes, fine. They nodded me out.

But then this spot—what does it mean? I ask. They don't quite answer: It's often nothing, the doctor says. We'll need to do some follow-ups.

It isn't necessarily scarring, he explains, clicking back, rechecking. They're often just—light. We don't know what.

These things are common, he says.

Lots of things are common, I say. It's not really a recommendation.

I can see the spot on the film now that they've shown me: a shard of mica, a fleck.

It could just disappear, as if none of this ever happened, the doctor says.

The mind is mute, a fruit held in the shell of the skull: a brain has made a machine to which the brain is mere fruit. That spot is a bruising; no, a ripening; no, a silver thread of vision coiled on the mind's surface, curled like a caterpillar in the grooves. Grooves that circle back under, go nowhere but into the firm curve of the spine. They will look at the results then call me. They will say nothing of what they can see in them other than: Should I fear? Never, should I love, should I hope?

Never: we saw in the poise of the head on the neck, your pride; in the tilt of the chin, your humility.

We saw: anything born nested in this gray must beat itself against bone.

No, they stand to look at my chart; flick the light on behind the film; turn back and have a look at me.

Probably nothing to worry about, they say. Try not to worry.

·

The next day on my morning walk, through the cemetery, by the farmland along the river, I notice: it isn't even quiet here anymore, cars passing constantly. But this is my walk, my habit, to cut through the old graveyard and follow the trail by the river, tripping a little, the earth here is soft and tufted, so many small hillocks—nothing sinister, the land by the river has always been like this.

# A

I picked a moth up off the floor. It was nearly dead and I waited, watched. It seemed as alien as anything could be and still have a name. On the back of its thorax was a design, black and gray and green accented, I think meant to look like a face, to confuse. I watched this false face: that's what it's there for.

I think I have the wrong kind of mercy. I'll slide a piece of paper under the legs of any spider and free it in the garden. Even in winter when I know it will die there.

I lay mousetraps but I won't check them, Vivienne does it for me whenever she visits.

You don't mind? I ask her.

I mind, but I don't mind minding, she says.

·

After Jay died, F and I used to see his parents often, or it seemed often to us. We'd have dinner with them and they'd tell us Jay was going to be in this book, on that website. We started to see stories about Jay everywhere, his parents talking in radio interviews, online clips. They kept F out of it because he'd insisted, they only said: he picked Jay up then, at this clinic, when Jay tried to leave our younger son fought him back in. I remembered the bruise on F's cheekbone. I'd watched it pass through all the colors.

We're going to this march, F's parents would say to us. Why don't you come?

We would go, but we wouldn't tell them. F liked this idea, that we might turn in the midst of a crowd and happen to see them. As though to tell them, you are no more than this to me, someone happened upon. We're all here, in the heat, lined up according to permits along certain streets, and it won't do a thing. The war ended in its own time, Jay in his, nothing to do with us, nothing to do with each other.

What I said to F: each coin had borne the face of the fallen leader, each would have to be replaced.

I could have reached across the coffee table, taken F's mother by the hand. Said that if it would have done anything we'd have filled that recruiting center with pig's blood, effaced every name in the files, hundreds who would not have gone to war because of us.

Or: sat outside the right building gas-doused and set ourselves aflame.

·

Did you know? Ford's parents asked us when Z died. Did you know what he was doing?

No.

I didn't point out to Ford after, what luck in phrasing, that we could answer this honestly. F would have been disgusted—what does that matter? he'd have said. We'll lie to them, to anyone, forever. You know that.

.

I send flowers on the anniversary of Jay's death, to Ford and his parents. I don't know if they'd rather I didn't, if they are trying to learn not to remember. I have the wrong kind of compassion.

.

The night Z died, I wanted to write about it, but we were left with too many words. When we should have had one history.

.

Suicide or accident? This was everyone's question. No one could say. Z had left this choice for us, though he had executed everything up to that point. Had ended his story otherwise so neatly: not a loose end, no evidence that could link him to anyone. Nothing that could say conclusively: accident or—? It was probably an accident, the authorities said, refusing final judgment: although he would have had time to move back, they always added; it's hard to understand, if he hadn't stayed so close he would have survived. So where does this leave us? we demanded of them, of each other. Between two words, impossibly. Did he mean only this small task for us, to choose one word to call him by?

That night we kept our eyes on each other's faces, watched for some reflection, that someone might finally say—

Then it was day, we got up, we went on. We might have wished for some trace: a red stain on the forehead from praying. Nothing.

.

But I have the wrong kind of memory, able to hold two truths at once. Whole histories have fallen from me, the motion of the neck breaking.

I stand still to watch leaves fall on a car windshield.

The war slips from the news. In time, from me. How can I remember what I never knew? The papers say less and less. An election, another series of bombs. Mentioned in passing.

They say it is a resilient country. The blast walls hold around the main ministries. Men smoke in cafés on street corners, tobacco scented with apples. Electricity steadies. The refugees do not return.

.

Zechariah's hand was thrown toward the wall as he fell. As though offering. That's how it looked in the photo they took. But this at least must have been only accident, a body arranged in falling. It would be wrong to believe otherwise. Look to Z's namesake: father of a prophet, yet of his death they said only that he was slain between sanctuary and altar. And warned the next generation that blood shed in the past would be visited upon them.

# Acknowledgments

For background on and analysis of the US war in Iraq, and for reporting many of the incidents that appear in this novel, I am indebted to the following works (in alphabetical order):

Iraq Veterans Against the War and Aaron Glantz, *Winter Soldier Iraq and Afghanistan: Eyewitness Accounts of the Occupations*, foreword by Anthony Swofford (Chicago: Haymarket Books, 2008). Dahr Jamail, *Beyond the Green Zone: Dispatches from an Unembedded Journalist in Occupied Iraq*, foreword by Amy Goodman and Denis Moynihan (Chicago: Haymarket Books, 2007). Nir Rosen, *The Triumph of the Martyrs: A Reporter's Journey into Occupied Iraq* (Washington, DC: Potomac Books, 2008; first edition published as *In the Belly of the Green Bird: The Triumph of the Martyrs in Iraq* by Free Press, 2006). Anthony Shadid, *Night Draws Near: Iraq's People in the Shadows of America's War* (New York: Henry Holt, 2005; New York: Picador, 2006). Müge Gürsoy Sökmen, ed., *World Tribunal on Iraq: Making the Case Against War*, forewords by Arundhati Roy and Richard Falk (Northampton,

MA: Olive Branch Press, 2008). Elise Tripp, ed., *Surviving Iraq: Soldiers' Stories* (Northampton, MA: Olive Branch Press, 2007).

The following articles deserve special mention: Mark Danner, "US Torture: Voices from the Black Sites," *New York Review of Books* 56.6 (9 April 2009). Erica Goode, "After Combat, Victims of an Inner War," *New York Times* (2 August 2009). Ann Jones, "Iraq's Invisible Refugees," *Nation* (9 March 2009). Joshua Kors, "How the VA Abandons Our Vets," *Nation* (15 September 2008). Joshua Kors, "Disposable Soldiers," *Nation* (26 April 2010). Nir Rosen, "An Ugly Truth: What Changed in Iraq," *Boston Review* (November/December 2009). Marc Santora, "Pullout from Iraq Faces Daunting Challenges," *New York Times* (9 October 2009). Timothy Williams and Suadad al-Salhy, "Fate of Iraqis Gone Missing Haunts Those Left Behind," *New York Times* (25 May 2009). Edward Wong, "Iraq's Curse: A Thirst for Final, Crushing Victory," *New York Times* (3 June 2007). *Democracy Now!* and Al-Jazeera English provided years of essential ongoing coverage of the war. I apologize if I have neglected to credit a source that any passage of the novel relies upon.

Anthony Shadid's work was particularly vital. Like thousands of others I will miss his writing and mourned his untimely death in February 2012.

The title of the article that serves as prologue to the novel is borrowed from Douglas Robinson's "Townhouse Razed by Blast and Fire; Man's Body Found," *New York Times* (7 March 1970).

•

Thank you to the board members of FC2, for all their work, and to Dan Waterman and the University of Alabama Press.

Grateful acknowledgment is made to *Copper Nickel*, *Berfrois*, and the *Massachusetts Review*, where excerpts of this novel appeared.

I am deeply grateful to Zach Savich, Pam Thompson, Stanley Crawford, Etel Adnan, Jenn Mar, David Bartone, Jeff Downey, Jensen Beach, Kyle Flak, Jen Kleinman, and Karen Emmerich. Thank you to my family—Sydney, Terry, Trevor, Brandy, Berit—and to Michael Page. Special thanks are owed to Andy Stallings.

This novel could not have existed without Noy Holland. Thank you.